PRAISE·F

CW00815899

"This is a 5-star book in a 5-star
lights up the pages with his Alph

y

"Sweet, sexy, amusing, and unforgettable. Be prepared for another hot, sexy, and
humorous read."

—*Love Between the Sheets Book Blog*

"The chemistry between Blake and Jennifer is amazing! I felt like I was there with
them."

—*SubClub Books*

"Is it possible to love Blake even more than I did? A resounding YES!"

—*Goodreads Reviewer*

"Packed with more intense romance and suspense that will just blow your head into
the water. Amazing!"

—*Whispered Thoughts Book Blog*

"Funny, sexy and sweet. I love Jennifer and Blake."

—*Winding Stairs Book Blog*

"Aagh! I need more now! I love this series."

—*Twin Opinions Book Blog*

"Hot, heavy, steamy. On the wall, on the floor, everywhere steam!"

—*Three Chicks and Their Books*

"Highly recommend if you want a funny, sexy, quick read with a strong heroine."

—*The Book Bellas*

"I adore Blake! So many one-liners had me chuckling out loud."

—*Adriane Leigh, USA Today Bestselling Author*

"Blake will make you laugh out loud and wish you could have him with you in your
bed."

—*Arianne Richmonde, USA Today Bestselling Author*

"Should be called 'What a Man!' Awesome book. Incredibly sexy and hot!"

—*Amazon Reviewer*

BOOKS BY NELLE L'AMOUR

Seduced by the Park Avenue Billionaire

Strangers on a Train (Part 1)
Derailed (Part 2)
Final Destination (Part 3)
Seduced by the Park Avenue Billionaire (Box Set)

An Erotic Love Story

Undying Love (Book 1)

Gloria

Gloria's Secret (Book 1)
Gloria's Revenge (Book 2)
Gloria's Forever (Book 2.5)

That Man Trilogy

THAT MAN 1
THAT MAN 2
THAT MAN 3

THAT MAN 2

THAT

MAN
2

NELLE L'AMOUR

That Man 2
Copyright © 2014 by Nelle L'Amour
Print Edition
All rights reserved worldwide
First Edition: March 2014

This is a work of fiction. Names, characters, places, and incidents are either the product of the author's imagination or used fictitiously. Any resemblance to events, locales, business establishments, or actual persons—living or dead—is purely coincidental.

Nelle L'Amour thanks you for your understanding and support. To join her mailing list for new releases, please sign up here: http://eepurl.com/N3AXb

NICHOLS CANYON PRESS
Los Angeles, CA USA

THAT MAN 2
By Nelle L'Amour

ISBN-13: 978-1500399955
ISBN-10: 1500399957

Cover by Arijana Karcic, Cover It! Designs
Proofreading by Karen Lawson
Formatting by BB eBooks

To my A-list—Adriane, Arianne, and Artemis.
And my readers. I love you dearly.

THAT MAN 2

Chapter 1

Blake

I was playing with one of the snow globes my mother designed every Christmas—her special gift to all her friends as well as my father's. I had a collection of them on the credenza behind my desk. The one in my hand had a tiny angel inside. I shook it, and glittering snowflakes fluttered over the delicate sculpture. My mind jumped to another angel. A real life one. Jennifer McCoy. Her angelic face with those liquid green eyes and turned-up rosebud lips filled my head. I couldn't stop thinking about her.

It was almost eight o'clock. I set the whimsical sphere back down on my credenza and glanced out of my corner office window. The mid-December sky was dark and eerie with the full moon shrouded by a cloud. The taping of *Wheel of Pain* would be over soon. I wondered how Jennifer had fared. It was her first time overseeing one of SIN-TV's adult game shows. Producer Don Springer was a fucking lowlife prick, but he knew the rules. Never to fuck with network personnel. But I was worried. Jen was a nice girl, and she'd probably never dealt with his type before. In retrospect, I should have never asked her to do the job. Guilt and apprehension ate away at me. Shutting down my computer, I decided to head over to the set. To make sure she was okay. To be honest, I just plain and simple wanted to see her.

All afternoon, I couldn't focus on my work. My cock was twitchy. I kept thinking about my lunch with my bud, Jaime Zander, and his twins. Jennifer had joined us, and she was so damn cute with those babies. There I was contemplating fatherhood, and I'd never even considered myself boyfriend material. Yeah, I wanted to fuck her. But I also wanted to cuddle her. And talk to her. Why did I always have so much fun with her? I never spent any quality time with my hook-ups. They were just good fucks. I bedded them at my fuck pad and bid them good-bye. I felt different about Jennifer. She was special. Feisty. Smart. Ambitious. And funny too. So different from all the women I'd been with, even physically. My usual type was a blond supermodel; Jen was petite and brunette. Yet, I was insanely attracted to her. There was a chemistry between us that made me snap, crackle, and pop. I found myself eager to go to work just to see her, and when she was away from me, I missed her. Though I'd known her for only a week, we'd shared so much—including one unbeknownst kiss of epic proportions. The memory of that blindfolded kiss made my blood race and brought a smile to my face. The smile was fleeting. There was one major problem. She was engaged. To Bradley Wick, DDS. Code name: Dickwick. Alpha me had no idea how to defeat the enemy. And he was such a dweeb. Frustration gnawed at me as I packed up to leave.

I could have walked over to the studio, but it was late so I decided to drive. I'd probably split directly from the set and go straight home. Lately, I had no interest in going to my club and bedding my hook-up du jour; my coterie of regulars was not too pleased. Hopping into my car, it took me no time to get there. I pulled into the vacant spot reserved for me outside the building.

After parking my Porsche, I headed into the vast hangar-like structure. The paunchy security guard was dozing. When he heard my footsteps, he bolted to attention. Mental note: You snooze; you lose. Time for an early retirement.

Slightly flustered, he bid me good evening.

"Is everything all right?" I asked.

"As far as I can tell," he replied with a nervous smile. "Have a good evening, Mr. Burns."

With a nod, I passed through the entrance to a long hallway that led to the *Wheel of Pain* soundstage. As I neared it, a woman's shrieks sounded in my ears. They were clearly not coming from a contestant desperate to climax but rather from someone desperate and frightened.

"Stop it!" she screamed out, and in an instant, I recognized the terrified voice. Jennifer's. My heart thudded. I raced down the corridor. Fuck. Something was wrong. Very wrong. Another scream pierced the air followed by a loud wail.

Breathing heavily, I yanked open the door to the studio. My eyes grew wide and my pulse went into overdrive. Springer had her pinned down on the spinning Wheel of Pain and was devouring her. He pressed his husky body against her slight one, pawing and gnawing her like a fucking wild animal. Bees were swarming above them.

"Let go of me. Please!" she cried out.

Unaware of my presence, the monster sprung his shit-ass ugly cock from his pants and told her what he wanted to do to her.

Not a chance in hell. I sprinted to the wheel, and with all my body strength, I stopped it. Brought it to a sudden halt at my feet.

"You fucking bastard!" I yanked Springer off Jennifer and sent him sprawling onto the floor.

Daggers shot from my eyes. "God fucking damn it, Springer. You know the rules."

Red as a beet, he tucked his skank cock back into his pants and staggered to his feet. He sneered at me. "The bitch led me on. This was *her* idea."

I tightened my fists against my thighs so I wouldn't

beat the shit out of him or strangle him. "Don't fuck with me. This is not the first time. Springer, you're fired."

"Fuck you, Burns. There's no show without me."

"No problem. No show. It's cancelled. Get the hell out of here."

"You're gonna fucking pay for this, you fucking piece of shit." Zipping up his fly, he stormed off.

I immediately lifted sobbing Jennifer from the wheel into my arms and away from the angry bees. Her tearful gaze met mine. It was an unblinking combination of shock and relief. With her arms wrapped around my neck, she rested her head against my chest.

"Talk to me, ba—" I stopped myself before I called her baby. It felt so natural to call her that, especially cradled in my arms. Her mouth parted, but no words came out. I grew more anxious. Almost panicky.

"Jen, are you okay?"

Whimpering, she nodded. Her lips trembled and tears rolled down her face.

"Fuck. You're not okay. Did he r—?"

"No," she choked, cutting me off. She was shaking all over. Shivering. The bastard had ripped her blouse off. She was in my arms in just her bra—surprisingly a white lacy one. I took in an eyeful of her breasts. They were beautiful. Perfectly formed. Not too big, not too small. The size of champagne saucers. They quivered in the delicate fabric that encased them. I glanced down at her blouse, crumpled on the floor. It was clearly unwearable. Torn off pearl buttons were scattered around it, and I could detect a large tear by the collar. Her teeth chattered. The sound chewed at my heart, ripping it to pieces.

"You're cold."

Still trembling, she nodded again. I gently set her down and shrugged off my cashmere jacket. "Here, put this on. It'll keep you warm."

A faint smile ghosted on her face as I helped her with it. My fingers brushed her shoulder blades and skimmed her soft flesh. There was something so sexy about her wearing my jacket that was four sizes too big. She looked deliciously lost in it and so vulnerable. I badly wanted to take her back into my arms and hold her against me.

"Thanks," she sniffled. Her watering eyes met mine. "I'm sorry."

My eyes stayed fixed on her murky pools of green. "There's nothing to be sorry about. It's not your fault. It's mine. He's an asshole. Always has been. I should have never let you come here by yourself." I lowered my eyes in shame.

Her eyes reached out to mine. Something so raw and pure struck me somewhere deep in my soul as we stared at each other, our eyes half-mast.

"Am I fired?"

I let out a little laugh. "Yeah. Someone's fired."

She sniffled. It was the sweetest sniffle I'd ever heard. So soft and sensual.

"I understand. I'll pack up my office tomorrow."

I tilted up her chin and gazed into those oh so sexy sad green eyes. "Not you, tiger. Springer. It's been a long time coming. And I'm glad that piece of crap show is off my schedule."

She took a deep breath and quirked another little dimpled smile. "I guess I should be heading home."

Tears were still trickling down her face. I brushed them away; I couldn't help myself. The warmth of them heated my fingertips. I had the burning urge to lick them off as they streamed down her cheeks. Taste her on my tongue.

"You're in no condition to drive. Let me take you home."

"Are you sure?" She gazed up at me with those glazed green eyes, blinking back tears. God, she was beautiful.

My lips were ready with a kiss, but instead, I brushed a few silky strands of hair out of her eye. The fucker had pulled her ponytail out of its elastic. I noticed she was missing something else.

"Where's your purse and briefcase?"

"I left them in the control room. I'll go—"

"No, wait here. Don't move. I'll be right back."

I dashed up the stairs to the booth and, in a flash, returned with her belongings. I helped her sling her purse over her shoulder but held on to the briefcase.

"Thanks," she whispered.

"C'mon." Without another word, I wrapped my free arm around her shoulders. To my surprise, she didn't resist. Silently, I led her out of the studio, leaving the *Wheel of Pain* behind.

Chapter 2

Jennifer

The drive to my house was steeped in silence. My sobbing had subsided, but I was still shaking and felt sick to my stomach. Don Springer's sexual assault had unleashed bitter memories I'd suppressed. Left behind in college. Memories of being almost raped. They'd never caught my assailant, and maybe that's why there could never be any closure.

I stole glances at Blake. He steered the sports car with precision, one hand on the wheel, the other on the gearshift. I admired his handsome profile and noticed the length and beauty of his curled fingers. Though the convertible top was up, a shiver skittered through me, and I hugged his oversized cashmere blazer tightly around me like a blanket. Inhaling his intoxicating manly scent that permeated the soft fabric, I felt like I was wrapped up in him. I felt safe.

Noticing I was no longer heaving, Blake broke the silence. "Jen, if you're up for it, tell me more about what happened."

I told him about the stunt with the stinging bees.

How the poor naked contestants were in horrific pain and how I'd asked Springer to shut down production.

His face tensed up. "You made the right call." He turned to look at me. "Did you get stung?"

"Just on my hand."

"Let me see it."

I showed him my swollen left hand. The bee sting still smarted and was a painful reminder of my assault.

"Fuck. It's puffy. Are you allergic to bees?" There was deep concern in his voice.

"No."

He breathed a sigh of relief and refocused his eyes on the road.

As we neared the little Spanish cottage I shared with my best friend Libby, I apologized again. "I'm really sorry about tonight." My voice quivered.

"Stop it. I'm the one who should be apologizing. I should have gone to the taping, not you." He paused, his lips pressed tight with remorse.

I placed the palm of my bee-stung hand over his hand clutching the shift. "You came to my rescue," I said softly. "Thank you."

He twitched a small but appreciative smile. "Do you want to press charges?"

I wearily shook my head. "I just want to move on and forget it happened."

"Are you sure?"

I nodded. "Yes, I'm sure."

"Well, I'm going to make sure that prick never works in this town again."

We shared another stretch of silence and then I inhaled. On the exhale: "Blake, I don't think I'm cut out for this job."

He turned to look at me. "Bullshit. You're doing a great job. You made a tough decision tonight, but the right one. And everyone's excited about the programming you're developing for the daytime."

"Really?" It was the first time he'd ever given me a compliment. Well, at least about my work.

He winked at me and shot me a sexy lopsided smile. "Yeah, really." He turned his eyes back onto the road.

A tingly warmth radiated through me. It stemmed from more than the compliment because I knew from our lunch with Jaime Zander that my boss still wasn't in my corner when it came to my idea for a block of erotic romances targeted at women. It was more the way he looked at me. Those sexy blue eyes, that cocky smile, those cute little dimples. My eyes stayed on him as he turned onto my street. He knew where I lived, having driven me home from the beach over the weekend. My house with its rooster mailbox was the last one on the block, sandwiched between an empty foreclosure and a deserted parking lot.

He pulled up in front of it and parked the car. "Let me walk you to the door."

"No, it's okay," I said, unbuckling my seat belt.

"I'm fine. The lights are on. My roommate's home."

"No, I insist." My gallant hero hopped out of the Porsche. He circled around it and opened my door before I could crank the handle. I stepped out of the car as gracefully as I could, and together, we walked side by side to my front door.

I dug my hand into my purse and fumbled for my house keys. I suppose I could have knocked and had Libby open the door for me, but I didn't want her to see me with Blake.

I found the keys and found myself facing Blake. He was so close I could feel his breath heat my cheeks.

"Here's your jacket back," I murmured, awkwardly trying to shuck it off.

Placing his strong hands on my shoulders, he stopped me. "Don't worry about it. You can give it back to me tomorrow."

"All right," I conceded softly. The truth was, I didn't want to take it off. I wanted to stay blanketed in it as long as I could.

Leaving one hand on my shoulder, he tilted up my chin with the other. Little sparks coursed through my body as my eyes met his. I felt my heartbeat accelerate. My lips involuntarily parted as if they were begging for a kiss.

"Do you need a lift tomorrow morning? I can pick you up."

In my mind's eye, I fantasized running out of my

house, jumping into his Porsche, the top down, and cruising down La Cienega to our office as the wind ruffled his dark silky hair.

"Thanks, but no thanks," I forced myself to say. "My roommate works at Conquest Broadcasting too. She can give me a ride."

His brows lifted. "Who's your roommate?"

"Libby Clearfield"

"Ah, the researcher."

"Yeah." The inevitability of being interrogated by Libby shortly was nothing to look forward to.

A resigned expression fell onto his face. "Then, I'll see you tomorrow."

With a flick of my chin, he jogged back to his Porsche. Once inside, he put the top down. As I was about to unlock my front door, he called out to me.

"Don't get into any more trouble, Jennifer. I need you around." As he peeled off the curb, I let out a sigh.

Chapter 3

Jennifer

"What the fuck happened to you? And whose jacket is that?"

Bad luck. I hadn't managed to sneak into the house without avoiding Libby. That was hard to do when you stepped immediately into the living room—our hangout—as soon as you opened the front door. 1920s California cottages didn't come with grand entryways.

My redheaded roommate was curled up on the couch she'd scored at a flea market, drinking a glass of red wine. Her computer was on the coffee table next to the bottle and several scattered files. She must have been catching up on some work.

I slogged over to her, unsure of what I was going to say. I sunk into the couch and took a glug of the wine right out of the bottle.

"Did anyone call?" I asked wearily, eschewing her inquiry.

"Just Bradley to let you know that he was working late."

I sighed. Lately, my fiancé was always working

long hours.

"Okay, now spill the beans."

Reluctantly, I launched into tonight's events. Of how Don Springer had physically attacked me on the set of *Wheel of Pain*. Reliving every horrific moment, I told her how Blake Burns had come to my rescue. Saying his name made my heart flutter.

Libby was wide-eyed. "Oh my God! That prick could have raped you."

"Yeah, I know." Libby was one of the two people in my life who knew what had happened my sophomore year at USC. The other was Bradley. I never told my overprotective parents because I knew they would freak out and make me come home. Libby had encouraged me to seek counseling. That had helped me a lot with moving on and entering into a relationship with Bradley. Yet, as much as I had healed, the pain and fear that came with being an almost rape victim never fully went away. I was not the first on campus to be attacked by this sicko. Just one of the few lucky ones who'd managed to escape his vicious assault. Thanks to my pepper spray (which my parents insisted I carry in my purse), I'd fended him off. But now the memories of his assault were as vivid as if they'd happened yesterday. The stench of his breath. The weight of his body. The wool ski mask over his face. One word repeated over and over . . . cunt. And his horrifying signature— knifing off a lock of my hair. I trembled at the terrifying memory. Libby's voice cut into it. "You're so lucky Blake showed up when he did."

I nodded after taking another swig from the wine bottle. The Chianti seeped through my veins and had a warm, comforting effect.

"What made him come?"

Despite my distraught state, the word "come" made me choke. I swallowed hard. It was just simple, straight out question I was loading with sexual innuendo. What was wrong with me? It must be been the wine.

"I don't know," I replied. "I never got the chance to ask him."

I mulled over her question. Why did he show up at the set? He never said he was going to be there. Was he just checking up on me to see if I was doing my job? Or was there something more?

We chugged the wine until there was not a drop left in the bottle. "I need to take a shower and then I'm going to hit the sack. I'm exhausted."

I'm going to watch *Bones* and then call it a night too." My best friend loved this show, especially the quirky analytical lead character.

I wearily rose to my feet. "Oh, Lib, by the way, can you give me a lift to work tomorrow? I left my car at the studio."

"Sure. No problemo. See you in the morning."

Once in my small bedroom, I kicked off my shoes and shed my clothes. Before my bra, the last thing to come off was Blake's jacket. I took it off slowly, reverently, and inhaled it against my nose before folding it on my bed. I sighed. The heavenly scent of him was still all over it. It made me feel even more lightheaded than I already was.

Slipping on my terry cloth robe, I padded over to the small bathroom down the hallway and glimpsed at myself in the mirror. I looked confused and vulnerable. The memory of Don Springer fawning all over me, touching me in places he had no right to, sent a rush of nausea to my chest. I needed to take a shower. To wash the repulsive memory and touch of him off me.

After turning on the shower and adjusting the temperature, I shrugged off my robe and stepped into the checkered Art Déco tiled stall. I stood under the showerhead and let the hot water pound on me while I scrubbed myself all over with a large soapy sponge. Moving it to my center, I arched my head back with my eyes squeezed shut and pleasured myself. I managed to wash away the traces of the scumbag, but as I came in sweet waves, Blake Burns's beautiful face filled my head. I couldn't stop thinking about him. He had come to my rescue and held me in his arms once again.

I curled up in my bed, freshly clean and bare-naked. Wrapping Blake's soft cashmere jacket around me, I closed my eyes. Sleep quickly claimed me.

Chapter 4

Blake

I arrived at my office the next morning at eight o'clock and stopped by Jennifer's on the way to mine. She was already there. Sitting at her desk. Looking fresh and pretty. Her wavy hair hung loose and cascaded over a soft pink blouse. She looked exceptionally pretty in pink. Pussy pink.

Fuck. I had sex on my brain. I had her in my bloodstream. It was a lethal combination.

Something had changed about the way I felt about her. I'd seen her strength and I'd seen her courage. But last night, I saw her vulnerability. She was like a little kitten that needed sheltering. I wanted to be the one to take care of her. To protect her from the dangers of the world. From the predators and monsters who could harm her. I'd never felt this way about a woman. Caring about someone else was something new to me. I was the man *that* came to her rescue. I said it aloud.*"Thatman."* Rhymes with Batman. Okay, so I had a black Porsche instead of the Batmobile. But I was her superhero.

She gazed at me for a long beat and then acted as if nothing had happened last night.

"I've compiled a list of the bestselling erotic romances I think we should pursue for the daytime block and started on the PowerPoint presentation for Gloria's Secret. I also reviewed the treatments you gave me. My notes are on your desk, and your jacket's folded over the back of your chair."

"Thank you." I forced my voice to sound business-like. I could give a shit about my jacket but was impressed she'd gotten her assignments done on time given last night's trauma.

"Is there anything else you need me to do right away?" she asked, her voice sweet and innocent.

Yes, suck my dick. Jesus fucking Christ. She had me good. My cock strained against my slacks. Thank God, they were baggy in the crotch area because I needed the extra room. Having a big cock came with both benefits and baggage. Okay, mostly benefits.

"We're good." I forced the image of her luscious mouth wrapped around my dick out of my mind, and strode to my office. I slammed the door shut behind me and locked it. Once seated at my desk, I unzipped my fly and jerked off. Damn it. It was the second time I'd done that this morning. The first was in the shower. I'd woken up with a painful boner. Both times, I imagined coming inside Jennifer McCoy's warm, delicious mouth.

Fuck. I wanted this girl. I wanted her badly. My cock ached for her. My heart ached for her. But she belonged to another. That dipshit dentist she was going to marry. I'd never been the jealous type, but suddenly I was.

Twisting around, I slid the jacket she'd returned off my chair and put it to my nose. It now smelled like her. Cherry vanilla. I replaced the jacket I was wearing with the cashmere one. Anyway I could, I wanted to be next to her. Be inside her.

As the day went on, a queasy feeling overtook me. I felt sick. Feverish, lightheaded, and achy. Balls. I was coming down with something. Probably that damn flu everyone was getting. I'd had a tinge of it over the weekend, but I thought I'd beaten it. So much for super powers. I had my secretary, Mrs. Cho, fetch me some tea and took a couple of Advil. Neither helped. By three o'clock, I felt sick as a dog.

"I have great news."

I looked up from my computer. It was Jennifer. She was beaming. The sight of her got me briefly out of my misery.

She strode into my office and sat down in one of the armchairs facing me. My feverish eyes roamed from her head to her toes. "What's up?"

"The focus groups are all set to go in Las Vegas this weekend."

"Great." My voice was listless.

Jennifer knitted her brows. "Blake, you look flushed. Are you okay?"

"I think I'm coming down with that fucking flu."

"Oh no." She leapt up from her chair and circled around my desk. Her soft hand touched down on my forehead. A chill ran through my heated body. The good kind.

Her face grew alarmed. "Oh my goodness, you're burning up. Blake, you've got to go home and get straight into bed."

She helped me pack up, and half an hour later, I was back at my condo. Shivering under the fluffy duvet, barely able to keep my eyes open.

The next few days were pure hell. I don't think I'd ever been this sick. My body fluctuated between extreme chills during the day and raging fever at night. I was so feverish I hallucinated.

Jennifer McCoy was an angel who was sent down from the heavens to take care of me. Dressed in a cloud-white sheer robe with her long hair flowing, she floated over to me. Her beauty took my breath away.

"Oh, Blake," she said softly as she hovered above me and ruffled her fingers through my hair. "Let me make you feel better. Tell me what I have to do."

I moaned. "Oh, tiger, I want to feel your lips again

on mine."

She smiled dreamily and slowly lowered her head. Her lips touched down on mine. My back arched. They were silky petals. I nibbled and gnawed them as strength poured through my body. We moaned into each other's mouths. Her lustrous hair danced across my flesh and blood flowed to my dick. Ahh. She was making me feel alive again. Instilling me with potency.

My breathing shallow, I ran my fingers through her hair. It was even thicker and silkier than I'd imagined. Waves of satin. Another soft moan escaped her throat, and she let me deepen the kiss with my tongue. Her tongue found mine and followed it in a hot sensual dance—just like our first kiss at my club.

My cock grew harder. I gently pulled away.

"What's wrong, Blake?"

I traced her lips with my finger. "Nothing. I just need more."

"Tell me what you need."

I held her dreamy gaze in mine. "I need to be inside you."

She smiled and her eyes glinted with wonder and determination. Wordlessly, she stripped me of my pajamas, and then I watched as she shrugged off her gossamer gown and exposed her body. Her skin was unblemished porcelain, her abdomen flat and taut, and her breasts, two sweet scoops of vanilla ice cream with little cherries on the top. She kneeled between my legs, and her shimmering hair swept over her shoulders like a whimsical cape. In a word, she was beautiful. I cupped her sensuous breasts in my palms and kissed each one of her cherries. She tasted as divine as she looked.

She gazed down in awe at my arousal. Then in slow motion, she wrapped her fingers around my girth, barely able to make them meet because of my size. She held her hand there, waiting for her next step.

"Tiger, spread your legs and put it inside you."

Silently, she did as bid and slid my cock across her wet folds. I jumped when I felt the tip nudge against her pussy. With a thrust, I plunged it inside her, letting her guide me along with her hand. I felt her tight muscles clench around my hot, thick length. And then I began to pump in and out of her.

"Oh, Blake!" she cried out.

I woke up drenched in sweat. In my dream, I had made beautiful love to Jennifer McCoy, and she had healed me. But now I faced reality. I felt sicker than I did yesterday. Every muscle in my body ached, and I was depleted of energy. With the little bit I had, I rolled out of bed and staggered to the bathroom. I glimpsed myself in the bathroom mirror. I looked like shit. Like something the cat dragged in. I pissed, brushed my teeth, grabbed a glass of water, and climbed back into bed. I thought I was fucking dying.

Over the next few days, I barely got of bed. Not having shaved, showered, or combed my hair, I resembled a pathetic old cowboy in one of those low-budget Westerns. My hair was a rumpled mess, and a thick layer of stubble lined my jaw. The only thing I was missing was a broken in cowboy hat.

My mother's housekeeper, Rosa, brought me a care package every day, but I barely touched a thing. My concerned mother had called the family doctor, but he said there was little I could do. Rest and drinking lots of fluids were my best bet. So, I stayed mostly in bed, with my plasma TV on 24/7 to give me some company. I knew I was really, really sick because I was watching Doris Day movies on The Movie Channel.

My only other link to the world was my iPhone. I kept it under my pillow and forced myself to check my e-mails whenever I was awake which wasn't too often. I had told Mrs. Cho to circulate an e-mail, telling my staff to contact me only if there was an emergency. The Korean-born mother of four was turning out to be the best secretary I'd ever had. And I'd had many.

I longed to hear from Jennifer McCoy. I didn't. I sent her an e-mail letting her know that it was unlikely I'd be going to Vegas for the focus groups. She responded with a sad face emoticon. I returned the e-mail with the same one. The truth: I was sad. I missed being at my office. And I missed seeing her.

Finally, on Thursday, my fever broke and I actually felt a pang of hunger. I crawled out of bed and wandered into the kitchen. I opened the well-stocked refrigerator and pulled out a jar of applesauce and container of cottage cheese. I never ate this pansy crap, but that's what I was in the mood for. Standing up, I devoured it all. They must be super foods because I felt a hell of a lot better. I immediately took a shower and shaved, and then got back into bed. I reached for my iPhone and composed an e-mail.

To: Jennifer McCoy
Subject: Focus Groups

Please come by my apartment today at five p.m. to discuss the above. Here is the address: 10580 Wilshire Boulevard.

Thank you. —BB

I hit send. In a beat, she responded—she'd be here. I suddenly felt a hell of a lot better, but I wasn't going to let her know that.

At a little before five, Ms. Punctuality showed up at my door. She looked ravishing though a little fatigued in a little black pleated skirt and fuzzy white sweater. Her tortoiseshell eyeglasses were sitting on top of her head, and she was carrying her briefcase along with a large shopping bag. Her purse, as usual, was slung over her shoulder.

I was wearing my Turnbull & Asser blue and white pajamas and barefooted. "Hi, thanks for coming."

Her green eyes fluttered. "Sure. No problem. How are you feeling?"

Ushering her inside my apartment, I faked a cough. "Not so good yet. But I don't think I'm contagious anymore."

That adorable smile curled on her lips. My cock stirred. She looked me over.

"That's good. Where would you like to have our meeting?" Her eyes soaked in my spacious Wilshire Corridor condo with its expensive Italian furniture and spectacular views of the city.

Another cough. "If you wouldn't mind, I'd like to do it in my bedroom. I really need to lie down."

"Um, uh, okay." She was definitely taken aback.

She trailed behind me to the bedroom. I immediately hopped into bed and pulled the covers up over me. Taking in my vast room with its king-sized bed and myriad of boy toys, she asked me where I wanted her to sit. Her voice was shaky.

"If you wouldn't mind, could you please sit on the edge of the bed so I can see you."

An uncertain look fell over her face. She blinked her beautiful leafy eyes several times.

"Don't worry. I'm not the big bad wolf. I'm not going to eat you." *Although I sure would like to.* I bet her pussy was delectable. For the first time in days, my cock showed signs of life. I could feel it throbbing.

Hesitantly, with a nervous smile, she plunked down on my bed, putting her purse and briefcase along with the shopping bag on the carpet.

"What's in the bag?" I asked.

She relaxed a little, her face brightening. "I brought you a bunch of erotic romance paperbacks. Libby's handing them out to the focus groups and had a few extra. I thought maybe you'd like to read some. She reached into the bag and pulled one out. "This one's really good. And funny too. You might really like it."

I took it from her. *Beautiful Stranger.*

"Thanks. Very thoughtful." I tossed it onto the bed, knowing damn well I'd never read it.

"And you should try the first book in the series too. *Beautiful Bastard.*"

Now, there was a title I could connect to. "So, Ms. McCoy, please give me a rundown of the focus groups and your activities in Vegas."

Without wasting a second, she launched into the schedule she had planned over the weekend, which included observing focus groups, attending a book signing event, and meeting with various writers. It was hard for me to concentrate on what she was saying with her next to me in my bed. I had the burning urge to rip off every stitch of her clothing and flip her on top of me. My cock was in an uproar, but the thick duvet hid what was going on beneath.

She continued to babble on, oblivious to my arous-al. My eyelids lowered. And then I groaned. She stopped short in the middle of a sentence. Her eyes were wide with alarm. *Perfect.* I groaned again, this time louder.

"Oh my God. What's the matter, Blake?"

"I think I'm having a relapse." My voice was a raspy whisper. "My doctor said this could happen." I groaned yet again, this time adding a shudder.

"Oh no!" Terror filled her voice. "What can I do?"

"I feel so fucking hot." *Oh, did I!* "Would you be kind enough to sponge me down." *And give me mouth-to-mouth resuscitation.*

"Of course. Where's your bathroom?"

"Over there." I weakly pointed to a door opposite my bed and groaned once more.

She leapt up from my bed, and in a heartbeat, she was back with a large sponge in her hand. She sat back down on my bed and dabbed the moistened sponge on my face. She was so close I feel her warmth.

"How does that feel?" she asked.

"So good, Jennifer." Her touch was gentle and lov-ing. I longed for her lips on mine.

She palmed my forehead. "I think you're cooling down."

Not. I was heating up. Yet another loud groan. "It's like there's a fire in my body." *Raging in my groin.* I pulled the duvet down to my hips. "Jennifer, would you mind sponging down the rest of me?"

I sat up a little, and without a word, she helped me off with my pajama top. With each button she undid with her nimble fingers, an inner firework went off. A chain reaction of scintillating sparks. I lowered myself to my fluffy pillow and kept my eyes on her as she soaked in my bare chest. She was clearly in awe of my chiseled pecs, defined six-pack, and that perfect pelvic V that peeked out from the covers. Working out had its benefits.

Taking the sponge back in her hand, she began to run concentric circles around my taut flesh. Slow and sensual. I closed my eyes and moaned with pleasure. Beneath the covers, I had a serious boner.

"Oh, Blake, are you in pain?" Her voice was soft, a mixture of compassion and concern.

I opened my eyes halfway. "Just a little." My balls were aching and my cock was blazing. I so wanted her. *My angel.*

Shutting my eyes again, I let her rub away. She sensuously sponged every part of my upper body as well as my muscled arms. I savored every stroke.

About ten minutes into the body wash, I took the sponge out of her hand and sat up. "I feel much better now. I can't thank you enough."

Her eyes connected with mine. The air between us was charged with electricity. "It's okay. It's the least I could do."

"Why don't you stay for dinner? I have a ton of delicious food my mother sent over." *And breakfast too?*

Tension swept over her angelic face. She glanced down at her watch. "I can't. I promised Bradley I'd meet him for dinner since I won't be seeing him this weekend."

Fucking Dickwick. Every muscle in my body tensed. My cock sunk like the Titanic.

She gathered her things and stood up from the bed. I was too debilitated to see her out.

"You should stay home tomorrow, Blake. I'm sorry you won't be at the focus groups, but I'll keep you posted with the results."

"Thanks," I mumbled as she padded toward the door and disappeared.

I sunk back in my bed feeling sicker than I'd felt all week.

I couldn't get myself out of bed on Friday morning. I'd had a feverish, restless night of sleep. Not because of any damn flu. Jennifer McCoy was in my blood like the plague.

I stayed in bed all day. I opened that *Beautiful Stranger* book and read a few random pages. Of course, I'd have to pick the part where they kiss for the first time. I slammed the book shut and pulled the duvet up over my head and then jerked myself off. Would I ever be able to tell Jennifer McCoy that *I* was the beautiful stranger who she'd kissed blindfolded in a game of Truth or Dare?

At five o'clock, I heard the door to my apartment click open. Only one person had the keys. My mother. One short minute later, she was striding into my room with my grandmother by her side. Both were wearing jogging outfits, my mother's from overpriced Lululemon, and my Grandma's from now defunct Loehmann's.

"Darling, how are you feeling?" asked my mother, tidying things up.

"Eh," I grumbled.

The good Jewish mother she was, she immediately reached inside her monstrous designer purse and pulled out a thermometer. It was the old-fashioned mouth kind.

She hovered over me. "Open up, darling. Let's see if you have a temperature."

Reluctantly, I opened my mouth, and she shoved the glass column under my tongue. I pressed my lips together and made a face. I felt like I was fucking five-years-old again. I counted the seconds until she pulled it out.

She brought it to her eyes. "Ninety-eight point six. No fever, dear."

"Fever *shmever*," chimed in my grandmother. "I've brought you Jewish penicillin. My delicious chicken matzo ball soup."

I remembered today was Friday. Shabbat. I definitely wasn't up for going to my parents' house. Especially dealing with my whacked-out sister and obnoxious twin nephews.

"I'll go heat it up," said my mother, taking a shopping bag from my grandmother. She waltzed out of my bedroom, leaving me alone with Grandma.

"So, *bubala, vhere* does it hurt?"

"Right here, Grandma." I clutched my heart like I was having a heart attack. The pain was palpable.

She eyed my lower torso and pointed at my pecker. "And *vhat* about the *schmekel?*"

"It's numb," I replied glumly. Trust me, there was no pulse.

"Flu *shmu. Bubala,* you've fallen for someone." Grandma winked. "I bet it's that nice *haymisha* girl you brought to the house."

I grimaced. How the hell did she know? I nodded listlessly.

"Finally. You bring me some *naches.* Have you *shtumped* her?"

Only my audacious Grandma would want to know if I'd fucked her. I shook my head.

"*Vhat* are you *vaiting* for?"

"Grandma, I can't. Remember? She's engaged."

Grandma made a disgusted phlegmy sound and dismissively waved her veined hand at me. Before I could say another word, my mother reappeared with a piping hot bowl of soup on a silver tray.

Grandma jumped in. *"Bubala,* have a *bissel.* Chicken soup is good for the soul." She winked at me again. "And the *shmeckel* too."

My mother set the tray down on my lap. With a spoon, I took a sip of the delicious broth. Two hours later, I was back to my old self on a plane heading to Las Vegas.

Chapter 5

Jennifer

The days following the incident with Don Springer were beyond awful. I regressed to having nightmares. The ones that had haunted me in college. Always the same. A faceless monster attacking me. Knocking me to the cold ground. Groping and squeezing my breasts and between my thighs. Snipping my hair. Me fighting him off. Writhing. Screaming. The monster roaring cunt, cunt, cunt. Over and over until my eyes flashed open, and I found myself drenched in cold sweat.

But it was more than just the nightmares. I felt a terrible aloneness. Bradley, with whom I didn't share the Springer encounter, was working long hours and hardly had time for me; I guess his practice was booming. And Blake was home sick with the flu that had been going around the office. His stoic secretary, Mrs. Cho, sent an e-mail to the entire staff telling us not to contact him unless it was a dire emergency. I missed him terribly.

I busied myself with my work and prepared for my

first business trip. I was going to Las Vegas. In doing research for the block of women-friendly erotic programming I wanted to develop, I'd discovered there was big erotic book signing event taking place there that would give me the opportunity to meet with many authors and pitch them my idea. Contacting the authors via their Facebook pages, I lucked out. They were all excited about developing their novels into television series and couldn't wait to meet me.

When I told Libby about my trip, a brainstorm clicked in her active mind. "Why don't we kill two birds with one stone? There's a great research facility in Vegas. I can set up focus groups there and prove to your arrogant boss once and for all there's a demand for such programming. We'll have a blast together in Sin City."

Libby's idea made a lot of sense, and it would be super fun to go with her to Vegas, a city I'd never been to before. There was one downside: I was going to be on my own. Blake Burns wasn't coming along because he was still sick. There was no way we could cancel the groups because too much was at stake, and an opportunity to combine the book signing and groups wouldn't come along again for a long time. It was just as well. I didn't need him breathing down my neck. And I didn't need him wreaking havoc with my mind—and body. I was having only one problem with my job—my devastating boss. All day long, every cell in my body danced with tingles. I couldn't stop thinking about him.

Libby and I left directly from work Friday evening on a flight from LAX. The travel time took less than an hour. We were staying at the Hard Rock Hotel where the book signing event was taking place over the weekend.

Vegas was something out of a surreal dream. Libby insisted our cab driver take us down The Strip before dropping us off at the Hard Rock, which was located off the beaten path. I'd seen photos of Vegas and had even seen the city featured in movies and television shows, but nothing prepared me for the experience of being there. As we cruised down the famous stretch, my eyes took in both the elegant and garish hotels that lined it. I was in awe of how each hotel tried to outdo the other with size, lighting, and special effects. Tomorrow night, Libby wanted to take me exploring, but tonight we mutually agreed to settle into our rooms and call it a night as we had a big day ahead tomorrow. One thing about Libby, she would never put pleasure before work. She took her job very seriously and was the consummate professional. These focus groups were as important to her as they were to me.

The Hard Rock Hotel was vast. After checking in, we wove our way through the loud, dark, frenetic casino, my eyes wide at the sight of people throwing money into slot machines and onto gaming tables. I felt intimidated. I was definitely out of my element. I was happy to get to my room, switch into my fuzzy SpongeBob pajamas, and settle into the comfy king-sized bed with my computer to review the meetings I'd set up. Though he wasn't going to be here, I wanted to prove to my boss that I was professional and organized.

Just as I was about to turn off the light by my bed and call it a night, my cell phone rang. I didn't recognize the private number. But I recognized the voice. Blake!

"I'm here," he breathed into the phone, his voice sultry.

"What do you mean?" I was stunned and confused.

"Just what I said. I'm downstairs."

"I thought you were sick."

"I'm better. Have you ever gambled?"

"No." My voice wavered.

"Then get your sweet ass down here and meet me at the front desk. Let's see if we can make some money together."

Quickly donning a pair of jeans, heels, and an open-necked silk blouse, I headed downstairs to the casino. Sure enough, there he was, dressed in an elegant dark suit and open black dress shirt, leaning—or should I say posing—against the check-in counter. God, he looked sexy. My heart did little flips.

His mouth twisted into that cocky lopsided smile when he caught sight of me. My heartbeat quickened and butterflies fluttered in my stomach. Anxiously, I sauntered up to him.

"Is gambling with your boss allowed?" I spluttered.

"I gambled on you, so I think it is."

Smartass. "I don't have a lot of money with me," I said, adjusting my shoulder bag.

"Then, let's start making some. Have you ever played slot machines?"

"To be truthful, I've never gambled. It's not my thing."

"Well, it's mine. I gamble on everything. Come on, let's try our hand on a five-dollar machine. Follow me."

A few minutes later, I was sitting in front of a slot machine, my purse on my lap. Blake stood behind me, his body brushing against mine. I watched as he fed a five-dollar bill into the machine.

"Go ahead, you can either pull the lever or push this

button." He pointed to a square "spin" button.

"Me? What if I make you lose?"

"Ain't happening. I never lose at these things."

There was a part of me that wanted to disprove Mr. Cocky and a part of me that wanted to prove him right. To be his lucky charm.

Hesitantly, I pulled down hard on the lever.

Our eyes stayed glued on the spinning symbols—all of them pieces of fruit except for the number seven. I squinted as I'd forgotten my glasses.

"C'mon triple cherries," hissed Blake, balling his fists.

The spinning came to a halt . . . one number seven . . . then another . . . and then a third. All landing on the payline.

"Yes!" shouted Blake as the machine went ca-ching, ca-ching, ca-ching.

"What did you just win?"

"Triple sevens. The next best thing to the jackpot. A thousand smackeroos. Way to go, tiger!" He high fived me, his warm palm slapping against mine.

"Where's the money?" I asked.

"These days, you have to hit the 'cash out' button, and then you get a credit slip that you redeem at the cashier."

"Oh." I felt stupid that I didn't know that. In all the movies and TV shows I'd watched, a bucket full of silver dollars barreled out of the machine on a big win.

It wasn't quite as exciting the paper way.

"Okay your turn. I'll let you use one of my credits."

"Are you sure?" I didn't feel comfortable using my boss's money even if it was just digital dollars.

"Yeah. Go for it."

Wordlessly, I did as he bid, this time hitting the button instead of using the lever. My squinting eyes stayed riveted on the payline until the spinning stopped. A banana . . . an orange . . . and a lemon.

"What's that?"

"Fruit salad."

My eyes lit up with excitement. "How much is that worth?"

"Nothing."

My shoulders slumped and my heart sunk to my stomach. I was a loser. And I'd just wasted five bucks of my boss's money.

An attractive buxom blond waitress came by and asked if we wanted cocktails. Her goo-goo eyes on Blake were not lost on me.

"I'll have a Scotch. Ms. McCoy, what would you like?"

"Um, uh . . . water." I knew I shouldn't drink with my boss while I was technically on the job.

"C'mon, order something. We're in Vegas, baby."

Reluctantly, I gave in to a glass of white wine.

"Bet again," Blake insisted as the flirtatious waitress disappeared into the crowd with our order.

"I don't think so. I'm not very good at this."

"It's just luck." I could feel the heat of his body against mine.

Against my better judgment, I agreed to play one more round. I should have held steadfast because I lost again. Frustrated, I was happy when the drinks came. Blake handed me my wine and then reached for his shot of Scotch. He slapped a twenty-dollar bill on the cocktail waitress's tray. Her eyes grew wide and she smiled seductively. "Why thank you, handsome. Good luck to you."

Blake shot her a sexy wink before she parted. Why did that bother me? I swear the waitress had mentally undressed him. She was just his type—blond, stacked, and stunning. Was he going to hook-up with her later?

"To winning," Blake said, clinking his glass against mine and hurling me out of my mental ramblings.

I took a big swig of the wine. And then another and another while Blake imbibed a bit of his drink.

"One more time," Blake insisted after another sip of his Scotch. You know what they say . . . third time's a charm."

"Fine," I spat at him, loosened up from the wine. "But this time, I'm using my own money." Holding the wine glass in one hand, I unzipped my purse with the other and fumbled for my wallet. I pulled out a five-dollar bill and inserted it into the machine. I took another gulp of the wine and then slapped the spin button.

"C'mon triple cherries," I shouted repeatedly at the machine. Talking to the machine had worked for Blake. So maybe it would work for me.

My eyes stayed fixed on the glass screen as the spinning came to halt, and a symbol fell onto the payline.

One pair of cherries.

My heart began to race.

Two pairs.

I held my breath, and like in a slow motion dream, the final symbol fell into place. I couldn't believe my eyes.

Three pairs of cherries!

"Holy fucking shit!" cried Blake as a siren went off and a red light on top of the machine began to spin and flash. Crowds of people moved in on us, clapping and cheering.

"What's going on?"

"Jen, you just won the fucking jackpot!"

"I did?" I was in a state of shock. "How much is that worth?"

"More than a bowl of fruit."

"Like how much more?"

"Like five thousand dollars."

"Holy shit!" I could barely contain myself. Screaming, I jumped up and down like a child in a candy store, my arms looping around his neck. I was still holding my almost empty glass. Setting his Scotch down, Blake circled his arms around my waist and spun me around. Beneath the thin fabric of my blouse, I could feel my nipples harden against his steely chest. My lips were so close to his that they almost touched. I swear, I was a breath away from making contact with them, and if I'd had one more sip of wine, I think I might have kissed him. His lips were that inviting, and he held me in that position longer than necessary. Finally, he set me down. Our eyes never strayed from one and other. There was electricity between us. I could feel it and wondered if he felt it too.

"C'mon, Lady Luck, let's head over to a roulette table." With that dazzling dimpled smile, he clasped my hand. I didn't resist.

We strolled up to a table in the center of the casino around which two dozen or so spectators were gathered. Numerous players were calling out red and black numbers and placing large stacks of chips on various numbers. There was one available stool at the table.

"Sit," ordered Blake.

"Aren't you going to play?" I asked taking a seat.

"No. I just want to watch you play."

He anchored himself behind me, his warm breath skimming my neck. Tingles skittered up and down my spine. Blake handed the croupier my win slip.

"Hundreds, my good man," he said.

In a flash, the croupier placed several towering

stacks of black chips on the table in front of me.

"What do I do?" I asked naively.

"It's simple. Pick two numbers," he breathed in my ear.

"Okay, ten and thirteen."

"Why those numbers?"

"That's the date of my birthday."

"I'll have to remember that," he purred, fisting my ponytail. I didn't pull away.

"Okay. This is what I want you to do."

I was all ears. And all tingles.

"Take one of your chips and place it on the line between those two numbers." With the top chip of my tallest stack, I did exactly as he said.

Other players placed bets, and the croupier, a sandy-haired college-aged dude who seemed amused by me, gave the roulette wheel a firm spin. Everyone's eyes stayed on the little ivory ball as it spun clockwise around the spinning wheel, bouncing from number to number. There was tension in the air as the wheel slowed down. It finally came to a halt, and to my utter disbelief, the little ball bounced straight into the number ten slot.

"Ten is a winner," shouted out the croupier. Oohs and ahhs broke out among the crowd of spectators. I was in a wide-eyed state of shock as the croupier set a tower of black chips on the winning number.

I turned to face Blake. A big Cheshire cat grin

spread across his face, and his eyes glinted with amusement. "I just won, didn't I?" I gasped, clasping my hand to my mouth.

He nodded sheepishly. "Yes. A mere hundred dollars. I want you to play again and put everything on thirteen."

I gulped. He wanted me to risk it all? I'd won almost a whole month's pay. "Are you sure?"

He nodded again. "Do it," he commanded.

With jittery fingers, I complied.

The croupier gave the wheel another forceful spin and then said, "No more bets." My heart pounded and every nerve in my body buzzed. I chewed my lip as the little ball circled around the wheel.

The wheel slowed down, and the ball skidded across several numbers. "C'mon, c'mon, c'mon," I wished silently. My fists curled so tightly I could feel my nails. Finally, it stopped at ten again. Oh no! I lost. My heart sank painfully to my stomach—every penny I'd won was gone. And then, to my absolute shock, it edged into the next slot—red thirteen. I leaned into the table and squinted hard to be sure I was seeing things right. Yup, red thirteen. I even heard the croupier call it out. Holy shit! I could neither get my mouth to move nor my brain to send words to my vocal chords. A chorus of oohs and ahhs surrounded me, and I watched with wide-eyed stupor as the croupier piled copious stacks of chips onto the number. Several frustrated players left the table. From the corner of my eye, I thought I recognized someone in the crowd. Don Springer? A chill zigzagged down my spine, but he was gone in a blink. He was probably just a figment of my imagination, and I went back to enjoying my big moment.

"Holy crap!" I finally managed. I jumped out my chair and began to do a happy dance. Literally.

"I won! I won!" I shouted repeatedly, gripping Blake's shoulders as my feet did a jig. I'd never seen so many chips.

Blake placed his hands at my waist. "Do you know how much you've won?"

Delirious, I had no clue. "Tell me."

"About a year's worth of salary after the taxes."

"Oh my God!" I was close to fainting. Thank goodness, Blake was holding me.

Grinning, Blake drew me close to him. I could feel more than his rock-hard chest. Between his strong legs, that giant cock of his pressed against my middle. Goose bumps spread across my flesh.

"C'mon, let's go to a bar and celebrate." He pressed me yet closer to him and rubbed his hard length against my abdomen. My big win aroused him. And it aroused me.

My skin prickled. Temptation teased me. My mind screamed no; my body screamed yes.

"Just one drink. We'll talk business."

"Okay," I mumbled. "Just one drink. And only if you let me buy."

A triumphant smile lit his gorgeous face. "Sure. And besides, you owe me ten bucks."

Five short minutes later after exchanging my chips for real dollars at the cashier, I was sitting with Blake at a high table at one of the hotel's many bars. On the stage, some chesty redheaded lounge singer was singing a medley of Roberta Flack songs. I ordered another wine, he another Scotch. I craved something stronger, but I knew I shouldn't mix drinks, especially in the company of my boss. I could easily get sloshed and embarrass myself. That definitely would not be a good career move.

Our drinks arrived quickly—delivered by yet another disturbingly flirtatious blond cocktail waitress whose name tag said Kay. After again toasting to winning, we drank in silence. I studied his face. The flickering candlelight danced across his strong features, bathing them in a warm glow. I'd never faced him in this kind of lighting, and it awed me how spectacularly handsome he truly was. It no longer surprised me that he'd once been a model. He was the kind of guy who belonged on the cover of *GQ* and could sell ice to an Eskimo.

"What made you come to Vegas tonight?" I asked, fumbling for conversation.

"You."

"You don't trust me to do my job?"

"Of course, I trust you."

"Didn't you have a date with Kassie?" I recalled overhearing Mrs. Cho setting it up before he got sick.

"No. I had one with Kasey. She came down with the flu too."

Yay for her, I silently cheered and then mentally slapped myself. What was wrong with me? I was newly engaged and definitely not the mean jealous type. Or so I thought.

"Aren't you glad I came?"

"Tomorrow would have been just fine."

He looked slightly crestfallen. "Hey, if I hadn't come tonight, you wouldn't have won all that money."

I almost felt rich. But most of my winnings were going to paying off debts, including my car and student loans.

"It was just beginner's luck," I countered.

"There's no such thing as *just* luck, my father says. He says success is like a slot machine. You have to line up the three cherries—the right idea, the right time, the right person. If one of those three cherries is missing, you can't win."

I pondered his words, but the wine was clouding my thinking. It made sense, but I wasn't sure.

He glanced down at my engagement ring and then returned his gaze to my face. His eyes bore into mine. "Do you think you're going to succeed at marriage?"

My skin bristled. "What do you mean?"

"What I mean is . . . maybe the idea and time feel right, but is that dentist boyfriend of yours the right person?"

His question made my stomach clench. Fuck. I'd forgotten to call Bradley. I'd promised to call him the minute I landed in Vegas, but I didn't. But he hadn't called me either. Like what if my plane had crashed or I'd gotten into an accident?

I nervously twisted my engagement ring with my thumb. I couldn't answer his question. The truth: I was having my doubts. Yes, we'd been together for a long time—through most of college and grad school—and we both had the same goals of living comfortably and having children, but lately, there hadn't been much of a spark. Maybe that's what happens to couples who are starting separate careers or have been together for a long time.

As I took another long swig of my wine, the lounge singer began singing, "The First Time Ever I Saw Your Face," and a sad truth hit me hard like a hammer. I couldn't remember the first time I saw Bradley's face. Was it the cafeteria? In the courtyard? In a classroom? I just couldn't remember.

Blake held my gaze in his. And my mind flashed back to our first encounter in his office. How when he lifted up his head and met my eyes, I almost melted. I'd relived it so many times. The moon and the stars danced in my head. Inwardly, I quivered.

As if reading my mind, he reached across the table and ran his thumb across my chin. "Dance with me." Another command.

"I don't think that's a good idea."

"Please. It's just a dance."

On the verge of unexplainable tears, I bit down on my lip and simply nodded.

Blake rose and came around the table to help me off the stool. A breath later, I was in his strong arms, stepping slowly side to side, as the lounge singer sang the moving Roberta Flack song. So much taller than me even in my heels, my head just reached his pecs. I rested my cheekbone against his chest and let the words of the song fill my head. I felt the heat of his body and his heart beat in my ear. At this very moment, nothing else existed except Blake and me.

"You feel good, Jennifer" he whispered.

"You do too," I said back softly.

The song ended, and I pulled away.

"Well, I'd better be going. There's a lot going on tomorrow." I blinked once. Only once. We'd never talked business at all. My eyes stayed fixed on him.

He was about to touch my face, but stopped midway. He smiled wistfully. "Yeah." He paused. "Thanks for a great evening."

I quirked a half-smile back at him, the tears so close to falling my eyes stung. "Yeah. It was really fun."

Turning away from him, I hurried out of the bar before I made a total fool of myself in front of my boss. I didn't look back.

The truth: Blake Burns had given me the best time I'd ever had in my entire life.

Chapter 6

Jennifer

The morning focus groups were being held at a research facility in downtown Vegas—the early Vegas of the Rat Pack era that was now enjoying a resurgence. Dressed casually but professionally in black slacks and another silk blouse, I was sitting on a taupe brown couch in a small room, able to view the groups through a one-way mirror. A notebook and pen sat on my lap and a cup of coffee on the table in front of me.

The first group, women 18-34, had already started. Libby, seated at the head of a conference room table, was briefing a dozen or so respondents who were drinking coffee and devouring pastries. The women seated around the table were of various shapes, sizes, and ethnicities, and some bore tattoos. They came from all over the country, many here in Vegas for the book signing event.

Where was Blake? Though we hadn't made a plan to come here together, it was not like him to be late. I was looking forward to seeing him as much as I was dreading it. Everything was fine last night until I'd danced with him. Why did I do that? Wasn't there some kind of law about employees dancing together? Had I not drunk a couple glasses of wine, sleep would have eluded me. I'd fallen fast asleep, still swaying in his strong arms. Oh, he'd felt divine! The memory still danced in my head. I tried impossibly hard to force it out of my mind.

Libby, in her glory, started to ask questions about the respondents' reading tastes. The group broke into a lively discussion about books they were reading and authors they loved. Of course, *Fifty Shades of Grey* was mentioned, but so were so many others—Arianne Richmonde's *The Pearl Trilogy*, Adriane Leigh's *Wild,* and R.K. Lilley's *Up in the Air* series to name a few. There seemed to be no end to the list of books and authors these voracious readers devoured.

While two women were fanning themselves over a heated discussion of billionaire racecar driver Colton Donavan, the damaged hero of K. Bromberg's *Driven* trilogy (books high on my list to make into a SIN-TV *telenovela*), the door to the observation room burst open. Blake.

"What's going on?" he growled, grabbing a coffee. He didn't seem to be in a particularly good mood.

My eyes met his and my heart hammered. He looked sexy as sin—in a pair of faded jeans that hugged his long, muscular legs and a simple white tee that exposed his mountainous biceps and chiseled pecs. His dark hair was perfectly mussed up, and a fine layer of stubble lined his strong jaw.

"Did I miss anything?" he asked, crashing down on the couch, uncomfortably close to me.

"Not too much. The briefing and the books these women are passionate about. They're discussing them now. Libby is videotaping the focus groups so you can watch anything you missed later."

"Good." Blake sat back in the couch and stretched his long legs on the coffee table in front of us and his toned arms across the back of the couch. One arm draped behind me.

The warmth of his body radiated through mine. I immediately sat forward and pressed my legs together to quell the fluttering sensation that had gathered between my thighs.

I tried to focus on what the group was saying, but his presence was distracting me and knotting up my stomach. Why was he late? And why did he have that just-fucked look going on? Had he slept with that flirtatious cocktail waitress after I'd left him last night?

The latter question sent a shiver up my spine. Why should I care? I was engaged and he was a player. He had the right to fuck anyone he chose; I had the right to fuck no one but Bradley.

I forced myself to focus on the group discussion and engrossed myself in taking notes. Libby, as group moderator, was doing a great job extracting information from the talkative woman. In truth, it wasn't difficult. The enthusiastic bunch couldn't stop blabbing away about their favorite book boyfriends, as they called them. If anything, Libby had to work hard at controlling the group from getting out of control and talking over one another. The women couldn't spit out their opinions fast enough.

"Alexandre Chevalier. One word. Sex on a friggin' stick."

"Lane Wild. Holy hotness Batman! I need a cold shower."

"Jesse Ward. I can't get enough of that fucking crazy, hot alpha male."

"Drew Evans. Sexy arrogant man whore!"

"Remington Tate. One sweet, confusing, fucking hot beast of a man!"

"Ethan Blackstone. Oh my God! Sex in a suit! So smoking hot!"

"James Cavendish. Whew! I need me some Mr. Beautiful now!"

My body heated. Everything these women were saying mimicked how I felt about my boss. Drop dead gorgeous Blake Burns. My Mr. Beautiful. That these zealous women were confirming my programming instinct took a backburner position in my muddled mind.

I glanced over at Blake, soaking in his handsome profile. His expression was impassive. "What do you think about the group?" I ventured, butterflies aflutter.

"Except for the blonde at the end of the table, they're not very attractive."

Bastard. I clenched my teeth and balled my fists. I wanted to throw my notebook at him. Mr. I-Hate-Research was just not going to acknowledge I was right—that there was a voracious appetite for erotic television programming targeted at women. And then his cell phone rang. He picked it up after the first ring.

"I have to call you back, baby." He ended the call, and I fumed. Keira? Kirsty? Kitty? Kat? Or maybe that damn cocktail waitress. Her name tag popped into my head. Her name started with "K" too—"K" for Kay. I suddenly regretted spending last night with him.

Libby's zinger question enabled me to refocus my attention on the group discussion. "So, ladies, what would you think if some of the books we talked about today were made into television series and movies?"

The women broke into orgasmic shrieks. "Yes!" "Now!" "Holy fuck!" "Oh baby!" "Bring it on!" "I'm on fire!" These were just some of the words that spilled from their lips.

A smug smile crossed my face, and I turned to face Blake. His hands were tightly folded across his chest, his brows knitted together, and his lips pressed into a thin line. The look of defeat.

Libby wrapped up the group and handed the re-spondents their incentives—each an envelope containing a crisp one hundred-dollar bill for their time followed by a choice of a signed paperback from a myriad of books she scattered across the table. The women went at the books like sharks in a feeding frenzy. After thanking the ecstatic women, Libby joined us in the observation room.

"Well, I think this group proved that Jennifer's right—there's a huge opportunity to develop programming based on popular erotic romance novels. The next group, women 35-49, starts in a half hour."

Chugging his coffee, Blake rose to his feet. My eyes roamed up his fit body until they met his gaze.

"I don't need to see another group. Jennifer, please option some of these books and put development on the fast track." His voice was businesslike, bordering on gruff, and intimidated me.

"Yes, sir," I said meekly. I'd lined up the three cherries—the right idea, the right time, and the right person. But victory eluded me as he blew out the door.

Chapter 7

Blake

Last night, this girl had emotionally blue-balled me. She'd split from the night club and left me bereft. The cocktail waitress with the mother fucker big tits had propositioned me, and I could have had her. But I didn't want her. The only woman I wanted was Jennifer McCoy, and she wasn't mine to be had. She plain and simply walked out on me. My cock aching, I headed back up to my hotel suite alone and wanked off before collapsing into bed. The exercise was in vain. Another ache tugged at my heart that wouldn't go away. I spent a restless night, tossing and turning, wondering why this girl was affecting me, and woke up late in a fucking bad mood.

As if she hadn't pissed me off enough, now she'd mind-fucked me. Ms. Smarty Pants had just proven she was right—there was a tremendous, untapped market for erotic programming targeted at women, and SIN-TV had to be the first to tap into it. I called my father immediately after the group to tell him the findings before that know-it-all research girl got to him. He uttered three words: "Run with it."

I'd had enough. I wanted to get the hell out of Vegas, but I'd scheduled dinner with my Vegas affiliate manager at Valentino, a swanky restaurant at the luxurious Venetian hotel. I didn't want to cancel it because Vegas was one of SIN-TV's strongest and most important markets. Having time to kill, I decided I might as well check out the erotic book signing convention.

I'd been to numerous adult entertainment conventions in Vegas before, but this one topped them all. I was able to get into the convention hall with a VIP pass, evading the long line of women eager to get in. Many held copies of their favorite books in their hands while others held scrapbooks and Kindles in brightly colored fabric cases.

I couldn't believe my eyes. Women were lined up at authors' tables waiting to get their books and Kindle cases signed as well as to collect swag. These authors were like fucking rock stars to them. Except for a handful of male book cover models who'd come along for the event, I was the sole male in the vast room. I felt like any minute I would be tackled by a pack of man-hungry wolverines.

And then the inevitable happened. A voluptuous brunette, sporting a sinister snake tattoo, sprinted up to me. Her eyes lit up. "Aren't you Blake Burns, that famous model?" She was practically drooling.

"You've got the wrong person," I begged off.

"No, I don't. I've followed you on Facebook. It's you! Would you sign my Kindle case?" she asked breathlessly.

Before I could say, "fuck off," a hoard of women swarmed me. I frantically began signing Kindle covers. Damn. What had I gotten myself into? My eyes darted left and right in search of an escape. And then to my utter disbelief, one of the crazy women tore open her blouse. Out popped a pair of knockers that belonged in *The Guinness Book of Records*. Her puckered nipples looked like fucking walnuts.

"Ooh, would you sign my tits?" she cooed, literally shoving them into my face.

Holy shitballs! Get me out of here! And then I saw her. Jennifer. She was heading my way, wearing a what-the-fuck expression on her face.

Brainstorm! Faking a big smile, I feigned an excuse. "Can't. My girlfriend's on her way over. That's her over there in the black slacks and cream blouse." I pointed in Jen's direction. The women dropped their jaws and turned their heads in unison.

"Hi, Blake," said Jennifer, weaving through the swarm of crazies. "Looks like you've got yourself some fans."

Before I could respond, one of my fan girls hugged her and blurted out, "You're so lucky."

Jennifer scratched her head in confusion.

The wide-eyed woman zeroed in on her engagement ring. "Oh my God! When are the two of you getting married?"

Jennifer screwed up her face. "You mean to my fiancé?"

The women responded in unison: "Yes!"

Jen's expression grew more perplexed, her face flushed. I was enjoying every minute.

"Um, uh, sometime this summer."

I broke into a devilish smile. "You can read all about it. I'll post it on my Facebook page. Now, if you'll please excuse me, I need to spend time with her." I looped one arm into Jennifer's and, with my free hand, blew the lovely ladies a kiss. As I whisked Jen away, a chorus of sighs and pants surrounded me.

"What was that all about?" asked Jen, jerking free of my grip. She sounded more miffed than curious.

I answered with one word. "You."

"I don't need you to broadcast my private life."

I tugged her ponytail. "Don't worry I wasn't. I was sharing mine."

"Whatever." Furrowing her brows, she was clearly none too pleased.

"What are you doing later for dinner?" I asked, heading toward the exit.

"I'm going out with a bunch of authors. Do you want to join us?"

"Can't. I have a date."

"Oh." Her voice grew small and then she recovered.

"A really interesting idea came out of the second focus group. Which *you* should have stayed for."

Ms. Chastising emphasized her last words. Without reacting, I asked, "And what might that be?"

"A talk show. Something like *The View,* but hosted by a popular book blogger in which real women discuss their favorite books and get to meet their favorite authors."

"What the fuck is a book blogger?"

"Someone who has a website and/or Facebook page who reviews popular erotic romances. Some of these women have over twenty thousand followers. They could be extremely helpful with promoting our daytime block."

I had to hand it to her. She didn't stop at programming ideas. Her mind was full of ways to market and promote. Today, social marketing and promotion was everything.

She glanced down at her watch. "I have a meeting with one of the writers I'm pursuing in a few minutes. You're welcome to come."

My cock jerked at the word "come." I so badly wanted to kidnap her and take her back to my hotel suite. And show her what it *really* meant to come.

Swallowing a gulp of air, I responded. "Pass. Maybe we'll catch up later."

Unsure of what the rest of the day would bring, I let her go.

Chapter 8

Jennifer

The rest of the day couldn't have gone better. I met with one writer after another. A dozen in total. They were all so down-to-earth and excited to be part of the programming block I was developing. Over an early dinner at the Hard Rock Café, which Libby came to, I explained that I envisioned them having executive producer responsibilities, which would allow them to have input into the scripts and casting. They were in a word: thrilled. Wine and beer flowed, and by the end of the dinner, we were almost like best friends. I had learned a lot about this amazing group of writers. Several had been on the edge of bankruptcy before their writing careers took off while others had been in unfulfilling high-powered jobs. The road to self-publishing wasn't easy, but the rewards were well worth it. The pressure these women felt to please their passionate fans was daunting. Most were later judging a contest—The Best Male Abs in Vegas—along with the organizers of the book signing event. They invited Libby and me to join them. While party-loving Libby was tempted, we ended up politely declining and stuck to our plan of taking in The Strip. After paying the bill and a round of endless hugs and kisses, Libby and I found a cab and took off to the famed thoroughfare. Just as planned, we went hotel hopping. We started at the pyramid-shaped Luxor and ended at the magnificent Venetian where we took a gondola ride in a man-made canal. As we hopped off the boat, my eyes widened and my heart skipped a beat. Heading into one of the hotel's expensive restaurants was Blake Burns and on his arm was a tall gorgeous blonde. I'd had plenty of drinks but suddenly found myself wanting one more. I gulped past the lump in my throat. What was wrong with me?

Eager to leave, I begged Libby to head back to the Hard Rock. Reluctantly, she agreed with the condition we go to one of the hotel's many nightclubs. Libby was one tireless party animal.

The nightclub we ended up at was a karaoke bar. It was crowded, but Lib and I were lucky enough to get a large corner booth. Another one of those attractive blond, big-boobed cocktail waitresses came by to take our drink order. She could have easily been the sister of Kay.

"Have you ever had a chocolatini?" asked Libby.

"What is it?"

"It's like the most amazing martini ever. It's made with chocolate liquor."

I'd had a ton to drink. Mostly white wine. I didn't

think it would be a good idea to have another or mix drinks. I just didn't have the alcohol tolerance that Libby had. I'd seen her polish off a six-pack of beer at USC frat parties and then make it through several shots of tequila. I didn't know how she did it.

"I'll just have a cherry Coke."

Libby made a disgusted face. "Come on, Jen. We're in Sin City. You only live once."

"You won't be sorry," said the cocktail waitress with a smile. "They're delicious."

Reluctantly, I gave in to the drink. The waitress disappeared with our order.

"So, how's it going with Blake?" asked Libby while we waited for our drinks.

The mention of his name sent a shiver to the base of my spine. On the stage, a bad Lady Gaga wannabe was belting out "Bad Romance."

"Okay," I simply said.

"I bet he's reeling from the focus groups. The second group of older women was even more enthusiastic about your idea than the first. Wait till he reads my report."

Before I could say a word, the waitress returned with our drinks and set them down on the table. I have to confess the chocolatini looked amazing. Like a chocolate milk shake in a martini glass. And it was topped with a heap of fluffy whip cream.

After a toast to "us," I lifted the chilled glass to my

lips and took a sip of the creamy cocktail. Holy cow! It tasted as amazing as it looked. Rich and chocolaty with a nice little zing from the vodka. It coursed smoothly down my throat and into my veins. My glumness instantly lifted.

"Isn't it fucking amazing?" asked Libby after her first sip.

"Totally." I licked my lips and began drinking the chocolatini like it was chocolate milk. Before I knew it, I had depleted the glass. So had Libby.

"Let's order another round," insisted Libby.

"Are you sure?" Deliciously lightheaded, I craved another. God, was it sinfully good.

"Totally. Look at it as one of the perks of your job."

It didn't take much more to convince me. The cocktail waitress returned and we placed our order. She scooted off and I turned my attention to the stage. Some goofy-looking guy was singing "Blurred Lines." While he was no Robin Thicke, many in the crowded club were singing along and dancing to the lyrics. Even Libby was standing up and swaying her hips, totally into it. Not wearing my glasses or contacts, everything was a big blur to me. And the chocolatini hadn't helped. The lyrics sounded fuzzily in my head. Talking about getting blasted.

The waitress returned with our second round of chocolatinis. Libby sat down and proposed another toast. "To Blake Burns for giving us this opportunity."

"Yeah, to fucking Blake Burns," I echoed, clinking my glass against hers and then immediately taking a gulpful.

"Did I just hear my name?"

I gagged. I almost spit out the mouthful of chocolate liquid but somehow forced it past the golf ball-sized lump in my throat. Setting my glass down on the table with my shaky hand, I swiveled my head. There he was, in one of his expensive dark suits, looming above me. That dazzling cocky smile was plastered on his face. My mouth dropped open, but words failed me.

"Can I join you, lovely ladies?" he asked.

"Sure," said Libby who was totally nonplussed by his unexpected presence. I was still speechless.

"Scoot over, Ms. McCoy," he ordered.

I did as he asked and he gracefully slipped into the booth. I felt his hard, muscular thighs brush against mine. I took another large gulp of my yummy drink. In fact, I guzzled it. I finally found my voice.

"I thought you had a date." I didn't tell him that I saw him with his latest blond hook-up at The Venetian.

"I did. With my Vegas affiliate manager."

Was he was bullshitting me? The blonde he was with looked more like a porn star. Tall, leggy, and stacked.

"She had to leave early because her kid got sick."

"Oh." I still didn't know whether to believe him.

Diverting his attention to the stage, Blake began to

sing along with the karaoke singer. Holy shit! He had an amazing voice. A raspier version of Robin Thicke's. His body rhythmically brushed against mine, and every time the singer got to the "good girl" part, he turned to look at me with his smoldering blue eyes. A rush of heat spiraled inside me. And wetness pooled between my legs.

After the singer finished his rendition of the song and stepped down from the stage, Blake asked, "So, do either of you sing?"

A loopy Libby chimed in. "I have the worst singing voice in the universe. It can scare off aliens."

Blake let out a laugh. God, it was sexy. He turned to look at me. "And what about you, Ms. McCoy?"

Before I could say a word, Libby chimed in again. "Jennifer has an amazing voice. You should hear her."

Inwardly, I was cringing. Libby and her big mouth.

Blake kept his beautiful baby blues on me. They glinted with mischief. "I'd like to hear you sing, Jennifer."

"I don't think so."

"Ms. McCoy, I'm your boss and I'm ordering you to sing."

Fuck. Boss's orders. I chugged the rest of my drink. "Fine." I spat the word at him. With a triumphant smirk, he stood up and let me out of the booth. I sauntered up to the stage, but let me tell you, I wasn't walking in a straight line. I was smashed.

On the stage, I grabbed the mike and made my song selection. Katy Perry's "Roar." It was my favorite new song, and I knew the lyrics by heart having sung it in my car a gazillion times. It must have been the most played song on the radio. I'd even watched Katy's jungle girl video on YouTube several times.

At first, I felt nervous. My heart raced. Everyone's eyes were on me, including Blake's. But once the music started, my stage fright dissipated. I began belting out "Roar." I really connected with the lyrics. And Blake Burns really connected with me. His eyes never strayed from me. It was if I was singing this song just for him. Katy Perry, move over. I was going to let him hear me roar my way. Fierce and hungry. I was his tiger.

The song came to an end. The audience cheered me and applauded wildly. On cloud nine, I took a quick bow and when I stood up again, Blake Burns was giving me a standing ovation. Hooting Libby followed, and then before my eyes, everyone in the nightclub was doing the same. I felt as ecstatic as I did embarrassed. Thank God, I was totally smashed. I swept beads of sweat off my forehead. I had really worked myself up. Despite shout-outs for an encore, I staggered off the stage, hoping I wouldn't trip and make a fool of myself. That's what usually came with being Calamity Jen.

Dizzy with excitement, I wove through the congratulatory crowd and made it back to our table in one piece. Blake was still standing at the edge of the table, allowing me to slip back into the booth. Except I stumbled. Fuck. It had to happen. But before I went crashing onto the table, two strong arms caught me. Blake's.

"Are you okay, tiger?" he asked, holding me in his arms. His warm breath heated my cheeks. My blood whipped through my arteries and veins like a roller-coaster.

I nodded. I was a wet bundle of nerves. "I need another drink."

He held my gaze fierce in his. "You're quite the singer, Jennifer. Do you have any other hidden talents I should know about?"

His seductive voice sent me over the edge. "Blake, I need a cock—"

"Tail?" He finished the sentence for me. Truthfully, I wasn't sure if I could. His intense eyes and intoxicating scent were rendering me senseless. And weak in the knees. Breaking away from him, I slid into the booth. He followed me in, sitting closer to me than before. The heat of his body diffused through me. Under the table, my toes curled.

Our cocktail waitress came by again. She instantly shimmied up to Blake. "Hi, gorgeous, what can I get you?"

Gorgeous? It was if she only had eyes for him. I felt invisible.

Blake winked at her. I inwardly cringed. Why

should his every little move with other women drive me to despair? Get me some alcohol!

"I'll have whatever these beautiful young women are having," Blake responded before turning to us. "Can I buy you each another round?"

"Pass," said Libby. "I'll just have some water." That was a first.

"I'll have another chocolatini. In fact, make it a double." I could actually see daggers shooting out of my eyes, but the flirtatious, oblivious waitress deflected each and every one of them.

Libby looked concerned. "Are you sure, Jen? You've had a lot to drink."

"I'm positive," I shot back.

The waitress took off.

"So, Mr. Burns, what is it with you and cocktail waitresses?"

He shrugged his shoulders. "Nothing."

"Maybe it has something to do with the word 'cock.'"

"Ms. McCoy, I think that word affects you more than it does me."

I was tingling like crazy all over. Beneath the table, I crossed my legs to quell the unbearable sensation.

"Cock is a funny word," said Libby, joining our conversation. "I read once that it comes from the French word spelled c-o-q which means 'male bird.'"

"That's cockamamie," I retorted.

Libby burst into laughter. "*Cock*-a-ma-mie. That's a good one." She paused, that clever mind of hers clearly at work. "I have an idea. Let's play a game and come up with words that begin with 'cock.' The first person who can't think of one, loses and has to buy another round of drinks."

Oh, no! Libby and her games. My murky mind flashed back to the last time I played a game with her. Truth or Dare. A wildfire zipped through my already heated body. *That* man! That kiss!

Blake's dreamy voice interrupted my flashback. "Okay. What about cocky?"

That word sure summed up his personality. Of course. He thought with his cock. That fucking giant cock! The memory of seeing it exposed at his parents' Shabbat dinner flashed into my head. A shudder ran through me. And then a flutter crept between my legs.

Blake continued. "Oh, by the way, ladies, I should let you know that I never lose at games."

Fiercely competitive Libby smirked at him. "Neither do I."

"And, for your information, *Mr. Cocky*, I was an English major and excel at word games. No one can beat me at Scrabble, except my father who was an English professor."

Blake shot me a wry smile. "You should play with *me* some time."

Was that another sexual innuendo? Or was I just

reading into things? I mentally slapped myself. *Stop it, Jen. What the heck is wrong with you?*

Our drinks arrived. Blake proposed a toast. "To winning." Clinking my mega-size martini glass against his, I shot him a smirk of my own. I took a heaping gulp of the martini cocktail. Suddenly, my head began to spin. A din buzzed in my ears. And nausea rose to my chest.

"Whose turn is it?" asked Libby. The words spun around in my head. Libby's eyes focused on me. "Jen, I think it's yours. Are you okay?"

"Jennifer?" It was Blake. I whipped around and looked at him. There was no longer one Blake Burns but two. I was seeing double. Twice the gorgeousness!

"Jen, what's your word?" asked Libby, her voice impatient.

I gazed at Blake times two. I could barely get my mouth to move but managed one word. "Cockatoo."

Blake smiled that dazzling smile and I slurped more of my drink.

"You have a big cock too." I hiccupped.

"Fuck, she's drunk," I heard Libby say.

"I'm not drunk. I'm good."

Libby again. "Come on, Jen. I need to get you to your room. Can you stand up?"

"Sure." Grinning, I'm rose to my feet, and I felt the world tumbling down. My legs were jelly and my body was swaying. My hands gripped the edge of the table to steady me. My grin fell off my face like a scab.

"Shit, Blake. She can't walk. Can you help me get her to her room?"

"C'mon, tiger. Let's get you out of here."

A heartbeat later, I was in his arms. I gazed up at him, still seeing double.

"Did I win the game?"

"Yeah, tiger, you're the winner."

I held his shimmering eyes—all four of them—in mine, and then everything faded to black.

Chapter 9

Jennifer

I slowly peeled my eyes open, one at a time. Disoriented, it took me several long moments to realize I was in my hotel room. I felt like shit. My tongue was pasted to my parched palette, a God-awful taste filled my mouth, and my head was pounding. Fuck. How many chocolatinis had I downed last night? I'd stopped counting after the first. I must have consumed them like a bag of M&M's.

A ray of sunshine slithered through the blackout curtains. It must be morning. A loud knock at my door sounded in my ear. *Go away!* The knocking persisted, growing louder. *Okay, enough.* Tossing off my comforter, I staggered out of bed to see who it was. To my surprise, I was clad in my flannel SpongeBob PJs. I had no recollection of putting them on. In fact, I had little recollection of any of last night's events.

The knocking morphed into relentless banging. My fuzzy brain did some wishful thinking . . . maybe it was room service with a large pot of coffee—something I could really use. But I didn't recall placing an order.

With a shaky hand—God, I was hungover—I unlocked the door to my room and swung it open. Standing before me was Libby, dressed in a casual slacks outfit and carrying her large canvas messenger bag.

"Hi," she chirped.

How could she be so bright-eyed and chipper? She drank those chocolatinis too and, in fact, was the one who turned me on to that lethal concoction. Maybe she drank fewer than I did though she did have a much higher alcohol tolerance.

I struggled to liberate my tongue from the roof of my dry-as-a-desert mouth as she skirted past me and let herself into my room.

"I thought we could share a cab and go to today's focus groups together," she said, plopping down on my bed.

Reality threw a wrench at me. A wave of nausea rolled in my chest. I had another day here in Vegas to observe more focus groups and to meet with more authors. In my sorry state, I was up for neither. I just wanted to crawl back into bed and pull the covers over my head.

My tongue back in action, I headed back into my room, still in stagger-mode. "Can you wait ten minutes? I need to take a shower and get dressed."

"Sure. I'll check my e-mails." Sitting cross-legged on my bed, she pulled out her cell phone from her bag and began scrolling.

"Thanks." I stumbled over to my dresser and plucked out some fresh underwear—a pair of white cotton briefs and matching camisole—and then ambled over to the closet where I settled on an outfit similar to yesterday's—dark slacks and a pale pink silk blouse. I hadn't brought a big assortment of clothes along. Just basics.

"Libby, how did I get back to my room?" I asked as I laid the slacks and blouse across the unmade bed.

Libby looked up from her e-mails. "Blake carried you up here."

I gulped. "He did?"

She twirled one of her long sienna curls. "You were pretty funny last night."

The hairs on the back of my neck stood up. "What do you mean?"

"Don't you remember?"

A hazy montage of last night's events spun around in my head. Blake sitting with us. Me singing "Roar." All those chocolatinis.

"You mean the karaoke stuff?"

Libby laughed. "Hardly. You were awesome. Blew the competition away."

"Then, what?" My stomach churned. Maybe I didn't want to know.

Libby smiled wryly at me. "You got plastered and got off on the word 'cock.'"

"I did?" *In front of my boss?* I chewed down on my lip.

"And then you told Blake Burns that he has a big cock."

"I did?" *Oh God!* How could I say that? I'd never be able to live this down. Bile rose to the back of my throat as clueless Libby continued.

"Rumor has it his cock could star in a porn flick."

"I wouldn't know."

Blake's expanse of magnificence filled every crevice of my mind. The truth: I hadn't stopped thinking about his outrageous cock since the time I'd accidentally seen it at his parents' house. I gulped down another wave of nausea. In a state of quasi-shock and despair, I stumbled to the bathroom. I caught a glimpse of myself in the mirror. My reflection startled me. My eyes were bloodshot, and my skin was the color of okra. I looked as ghastly as I felt. The first thing I did was brush my teeth, to get the foul taste out of my mouth, and then I popped a couple Advil and downed them with a glass of water. Shedding my pajamas, I turned on the shower and adjusted the temperature of the water to as hot as I could take it. Maybe a hot steamy shower would wash away my emotional turmoil and give me clarity. I stepped into the stall and let the hot water pound over me. I squeezed my eyes shut. Oh, God. Blake Burns was back. This time standing in the shower with me, his cock—yes, his humongous cock—pointing my way. I snapped open my eyes and hastily turned off the water. If only I could rip yesterday out from the calendar. Make it disappear. Make *him* disappear.

As I towel dried myself and slipped on my undies, one reassuring thought crossed my mind. Chances were I wouldn't see Blake today. He'd made it loud and clear yesterday that he'd had enough of the focus groups and book signings. *Oh, please, no Blake today.*

I gathered my wet hair into a ponytail and had the misfortune of seeing my reflection once more. I still looked like shit. Today—with or without Blake—was not going to be a good day.

Back in my room, I quickly donned the rest of my clothes. I gathered my purse and my briefcase with my notebook and laptop inside. Before heading out with Libby, I reached into my purse. Seconds later, my dark prescription sunglasses were sitting on my nose.

As we descended the high-speed elevator, Libby chit-chatted about the upcoming focus groups. Yesterday's respondents were "heavy" readers of erotic romance novels, reading at least three books a week; today's panelists were "moderate" readers, reading, on the average, three eroms per month. Her cell phone rang. Retrieving it from her bag, she let me know it was from the research facility. Everything for today's groups was in place. While Libby spoke to the facility's director, I dug into my purse and rifled for my own cell phone. Poor Bradley must have tried to reach me while

I was passed out. He must be worried sick about me.

I scoured my handbag, but my phone was nowhere to be found. Shit. Maybe it fell out of my bag last night. This day wasn't getting better. When the elevator reached the main floor and the doors pinged opened, I told Libby that I was missing my phone and had to go back up to my room.

"Oh, I put it on your night table," she said. "Just in case you needed it. Hurry. I'll meet you outside the hotel."

Libby stepped out of the elevator, and I immediately palmed the twelfth floor button, the floor on which we were staying. Fortunately, the elevator made no stops. When I reached my destination, I slogged out of the elevator to my room. I should have sprinted, but I was still in no condition to move at more than a snail's pace. Every nauseating step was a painful reminder of last night's embarrassing debacle. I vowed I was never going to get drunk again. Or, at least, never touch another chocolatini.

I found my phone quickly and took a moment to check my messages and texts. To my surprise, there weren't any text or phone messages from Bradley. Not one. My heart twitched. Maybe something happened to him. I immediately speed-dialed his number. His phone went right to his voice-mail. Instead of leaving him a message, I texted him.

Call or text me as soon as you get this message.
I love you.

xJ

My mind wandered. Why hadn't he called or texted me? I told myself he must be okay. Surely, his parents or even his hygienist, Candace, would have gotten in touch with me if something terrible had happened to him. They all had my cell phone number. Maybe he'd lost his phone or taken a spontaneous overnight trip to some place where his phone didn't work. Unable to dispel my unsettling feeling, I tossed my phone into my shoulder bag and headed back to the elevator bank.

The elevators, this time, took their sweet time. This day just fucking sucked. Besides being still hungover, I was growing increasingly sick with worry. Bradley. The outcome of today's focus groups. Facing Blake.

I thought about taking the stairs—not a bright idea given my pathetic state and accident proneness—when an elevator car at last arrived. The doors parted and so did my lips. Standing smack in front of me was the last person I wanted to see. Blake Burns! Mortification raced through me. My heart was in my mouth.

He was dressed again in jeans, black body-hugging ones that hung low on his narrow hips, and one of those expensive premium cotton white tees that exposed his newly bronzed biceps. Dangling from his hand was an expensive tan leather overnight bag with his initials—

BB—monogrammed in gold. He must be checking out, heading back to LA.

"Ms. McCoy, are you going down . . . ?"

. . . On your big frickin' dick? Geez. What was wrong with me? I kept my gaze on his gorgeous face. He looked freshly showered and effin' sexy as sin.

"Well?" He was holding the door open.

"Um, uh, yes," I stuttered. A part of me wanted to run away or wait for the next elevator, but who knew how long that would take. Libby was waiting for me downstairs, and I didn't want her to be late for the groups.

Hesitantly, I stepped into the elevator. I stood as far away from him as I could and faced front. The elevator doors closed, and we began our descent.

"So, how do you feel today, Ms. McCoy?" His tone was sardonic, and in my mind's eye, I could see the smirk pasted on his face.

"Fine." I stabbed the word at him and adjusted my sunglasses.

"You were quite entertaining last night."

Every muscle in my body clenched, and I felt my-self flushing with embarrassment. "I'm sorry about last night," I blurted out, still facing forward.

He chuckled. "Don't worry, tiger. What happens in Vegas, stays in Vegas."

The high-speed elevator couldn't reach the lobby fast enough. When the doors parted, I darted out.

"Have a nice day, Jennifer, and stay out of trouble. I'm flying back. I'll see you in the office tomorrow."

"Bye," I squeaked, not turning to look back at him.

The focus groups went as well as yesterday's. Sobriety returned to me, thanks to the thoughtful research facility director who set me up with a pot of strong black coffee and a bowl of fresh fruit. After a quick lunch with Libby at a fast-food restaurant close to the facility, I headed back to the hotel to attend the final session of the book signing event. Once again, I met with numerous authors and bloggers who couldn't be more excited about the block of programming I was developing for SIN-TV. I had their full support and ended up with a bag full of signed books and swag.

Libby and I were booked on a 7:30 p.m. flight back to Los Angeles. With a few hours to kill, we decided to meet up at the Hard Rock pool. To catch some rays and swim a few laps. A margarita for her, a cherry Coke for me. After last night, alcohol was not in my immediate future.

While I was changing into my swimwear in my room, my cell phone rang. I quickly grabbed it, hoping it was Bradley and dreading it was Blake. It was neither. Instead, Libby.

"Jen, I got inspired to start writing up the focus

group report, so if you don't mind, I'll meet you down at the pool a little later."

"No problem." Work came first; this was a business trip, not a pleasure trip.

"Save me a lounge chair."

I told her I would and ended the call.

Before leaving the room, I checked myself out in the floor-length mirror by the entryway closet. For the first time today, I smiled at my reflection. Color had come back to my face, and the red spider lines had faded from my eyes. Wearing a turquoise one-piece bathing suit and flip-flops, I was back to being me. I slid open the closet and shrugged on the fluffy white terry cloth robe that came with the room. I was ready for a refreshing swim.

The pool area was packed. I'd never seen so much skin in my whole life. Women in string bikinis were mingling with hunky, tattooed men in Speedos or tanning themselves. Exotic drinks were everywhere. Wearing my dark prescription sunglasses and holding a plastic cup full of ice-cold Coke, I wound my way in and out of the crowd, searching for two side by side empty chaise lounges. At last, I spotted a pair. I hurried to them before someone else claimed them. Settling into one of them, I sipped my soda and took in the scene.

Three bikinied women, who could pass as triplets, with big boobs and even bigger blond hair, were fawning over a well-built, tanned man, lying face down on the chaise lounge next to me. A backward-facing baseball cap covered his head. One of the blondes was massaging his feet, another the back of his muscular thighs, and the third his upper back and shoulders. I recognized the latter—Kay, the flirtatious cocktail waitress from the other night.

She began to plant kisses all over his rippled back. He jerked.

"Hey, what are you doing?"

I gasped. The voice was muffled, but I recognized it immediately. Blake! *He was still here?*

In a state of frenzy, I leapt up from my chaise and sent my beverage flying, ice cubes and all. To my horror, it splattered all over Kay and Blake.

Shrieking, Kay scrunched up her face in disgust while Blake muttered, "What the fuck?" and rolled over. Our eyes met, wide in shock.

"Blake, baby, I'm sorry, I didn't do it," pleaded Kay. "It's all that little bitch's fault." She gave me a look that could kill. I felt my face flare and my blood curdle.

Blake bolted upright. "Jen, it's not what it looks like."

I took a couple of deep breaths. "You know what they say: what happens in Vegas, stays in Vegas."

With that, I stalked off, ready to get the hell out of Sin City.

Chapter 10

Blake

My flight back to Los Angeles had been delayed. With three hours to kill, I'd decided to hit the pool. I could use a little R&R. And a little sun. I had no clue I'd be accosted by Kay, that skanky blond waitress from the other night, and her two look-alike cousins, Kelly and Kendra, both Vegas showgirls. I'd told them to get lost (well not exactly those words), but they'd refused to leave me. I got stuck buying them drinks. While they savored their piña coladas, I rolled over on the chaise and closed my eyes. I was still worn out from my bout with the flu, and traveling to Vegas didn't help.

I must admit I didn't resist their sensuous suntan oil massage. These girls knew how to work a man. But while they rubbed and kneaded, I couldn't stop think about Jennifer McCoy. As I lay face down, a smile crossed my face. She was fucking adorable. She had the singing voice of the next *American Idol* and she was the cutest, funniest drunk ever. She was totally obsessed with my cock. But she also made me laugh. Have fun.

And yes, get hard. Hard as nails just with her smile. I'd managed once again to have her in my arms. A mere waif, she was so warm and delicious. Carrying to her room, I felt like her prince. And then, when I gently laid her down on her bed, she murmured my name in her stupor. My already hard-as-rock cock jumped. If her friend Libby hadn't been there with me, I would have kissed those rosebud lips. My Sleeping Beauty. At least, I was wearing her down.

But now, I'd unintentionally fucked things up. Bolting from my chaise and almost knocking down raging mad Kay, I jogged after Jennifer. She was taking angry giant steps toward the hotel entrance.

"Jen, wait up!" I called out after her.

Ignoring me, she quickened her pace. My jog sped up to a sprint. I was able to catch up to her. Gripping her by her shoulders, I stopped her in her tracks. I spun her around, and she faced me squarely. Anger flared in her emerald eyes.

"Let go of me, Blake. I need to get back to my room and pack. I don't want to miss my plane."

"Jen, I don't even know those girls. Honestly. They mean nothing to me."

Her eyes narrowed. "No girl means anything to you."

Her words were like knives to my heart. My hands fell off her shoulders. For the first time in my life, I was speechless.

She adjusted the straps of her tank suit and thanked me for releasing her. Her voice was as cold as ice. "I'll have a topline report of the focus group findings to you first thing in the morning."

With that, she stormed off leaving me in the dry Vegas dust. Maybe Jennifer and me were not meant to be.

Hanging out at the pool was a big, big mistake. Thanks to that regrettably relaxing massage under the hot as balls sun, I'd conked out. Besides fucking things up with Jennifer, I'd overslept and missed my damn plane. There wasn't another one available until late tomorrow afternoon. So, I was stuck in Vegas for another day. After my fallout with Jen, I checked back into the hotel. Maybe, missing my flight was a blessing in disguise. I could use the time away from my tiger to clear my head and figure out my next move. Our recent encounter had set things back. She simply refused to believe there was nothing going on between me and that trio of blondes.

I moped up to my room and ordered room service. I then texted Jennifer to let her know about my change of plans—that I wouldn't be back in the office until Tuesday. I eagerly awaited her reply. Zippo. She must already be on her flight back to Los Angeles. Or perhaps she was just ignoring me.

While waiting for my dinner to arrive, I called Vera Nichols, my Vegas affiliate manager. She picked up the phone quickly. Since I was going to be in town for another day, I told her I wanted to visit some of the SIN-TV productions filming nearby. Because of the new California law requiring porn stars to wear condoms, many of our shows had recently moved to Sin City where they weren't mandatory. It was just as well because filming in Nevada was a lot cheaper than filming in Los Angeles. Vera was extremely receptive to the idea and told me she would pick me up in the morning. I was glad she was coming along. Vera was a great gal and I could use the company.

Room service arrived. I checked my phone. Still no response from Jennifer. After a few bites of my steak, I took a quick shower and went straight to sleep. I was too despondent to jerk myself off.

Monday morning, bright and early, Vera picked me up in her red Mustang convertible. Driving at eighty miles an hour, we were out of Vegas in no time, cruising down a newly built highway. At this hour, there were hardly any cars on the road. Vera was taking me to a remote area where many of our shows had set up production. The already warm dry desert wind blew against my face while I soaked in the scenery. I'd never actually been out of Vegas before and was in awe of the beauty of the desert wildlife and rocky terrain. The next frontier, I mused. It was only a matter of time until someone like Steve Wynn laid his stake in this virgin ground and built a brand new strip of luxury hotels and casinos.

"How's your son doing?" I asked Vera.

"Much better." She smiled. "I thought he was coming down with the flu but it turned out to be just a twenty-four-hour bug."

"That's lucky. I had that flu last week and it sucked." The memory of Jennifer coming to my apartment and taking care of me flashed into my head. Despite the pleasant temperature, it sent a shiver straight to my dick.

"Kids are such a joy, but they come with so much responsibility. Being a parent is the hardest job you'll ever love," she added with a laugh.

"I wouldn't know." And, at the rate my love life was going, I might never know. Jennifer, however, was marrying that dweeb dentist Bradley, and I wouldn't be surprised if she had a family before long. That fucking anal Dickwick probably had things all planned out. I inwardly groaned. *Operation Dickwick* was sadly at a standstill.

About a half an hour into the ride, my cell phone buzzed. A text. Holding it in my hand, I quickly checked whom it was from. My heartbeat quickened. It was from Jennifer. Two cold little letters responding to my text from last night: *ok*. My heart sank. She didn't even fucking take the time to capitalize the "o." So much of me was hoping she would have written something like: *Looking forward to seeing you on Tuesday*. That and a little *xo*.

With Jennifer on my mind and in my heart, I told Vera about her idea for a daytime block targeted at women as well as about the focus groups and erotica book signing. Keeping her eyes on the road, she listened intently. When I was done, she repeated verbatim the words my father had used, "Mommy porn. That's fucking brilliant."

I could trust Vera. She was my favorite affiliate manager. In her late thirties, she was strong yet compassionate and didn't take shit from anyone. Raised by her single-parent mother, an abusive drug-addicted showgirl, she'd managed to get both a college degree and business degree. She was married to a great guy who designed neon signs for Vegas hotels. Tall, blond, and beautiful, she reminded me in many ways of Gloria Zander. I admired her greatly, like I did Gloria.

"Your new development girl sounds like a rare find," commented Vera as we came upon what looked like a studio in the middle of the desert.

"She is," I breathed.

For the first time on our drive, Vera turned her head to look at me. "Blake Burns, I detect some feelings in your voice." She gave me a knowing smile. "Do you more than like her?"

I let out a loud exasperated sigh. "Yeah, I do. I've never met anyone like her before."

"So what's stopping you, Blake? You know Conquest is pretty liberal when it comes to interoffice affairs."

"She doesn't trust me."

Vera laughed lightly. "Well, Mr. Hook-Up, I can understand that."

I scowled, but she had a point. "It's more than that. She's engaged."

I expected her eyes to shoot up, but they didn't. Instead, she smiled warmly. "I never told you this, but I was engaged when I met Steve."

"Really?" Steve was her beloved husband.

"Yup. It was love at first sight. It took me a bit, but I broke off my engagement with my fiancé whom I realized was not the right man for me. I've never looked back."

My heartbeat sped up, in a good way. Vera had instilled in me some guarded optimism. Hope. Maybe, Jennifer did have feelings for me, but didn't know to handle them. I mean, at times the electricity between the two of us was palpable. Sparks had flown in the air we breathed. I just needed to figure out how to prove that I was better for her than fucking Dickwick. I thought back to Jaime Zander's words of wisdom. I needed to romance her. Shower her with compliments. Buy her presents. I bet the cheapskate bought her *bubkus.* I mean, that ring was a total joke. I immediately called my secretary, Mrs. Cho, and asked her to arrange a flower delivery to Jennifer McCoy. A dozen red roses with a note from me. *Thanks for a great job— Blake* But before hanging up, I had an even better idea. I told Mrs. Cho to instead call my mother's exotic florist and have a large flowering cactus plant delivered to Jennifer's office. So much more fitting. Phallic. And symbolic. And it would last a lot longer than the roses if Jennifer took proper care of it. Maybe forever.

Vera smiled warmly. "You're very good, Blake. Don't lose hope."

"Thanks," I said as she pulled into the parking lot of the studio. "What show is this?"

"Private Dick." Great. My favorite show on our schedule. I loved the lead character. Oral Covert, the detective with the twelve-inch dick. My mind flashed back to the time Jennifer watched it with me in my office and told me it was *vomiticious.* Her made up word. I laughed silently. And then my cock twitched. Eureka! I just had to prove to her that Dickwick was *vomiticious.* Yes, it was as simple as that. My father always said, "Where there's a will, there's a way." Whatever it took, I was going to find a way. My silent laugh grew evil.

The filming of *Private Dick* bored the shit out of me. I had no patience for the constant takes and retakes. Rod Hammer, the actor who played Oral, kept forgetting his lines and lost his erection every time the show went down. Everyone on the set had to sit around while he thumbed through a girlie magazine to get it back up. Jesus Christ. So much for America's most popular porn star and hero to millions. And if that wasn't bad enough, Pussy Amour, who played the hooker, Daisy, Oral's on and off love interest, was a bull dyke who kept complaining about her co-star's bad breath. In a rage, she threatened the producer, Eddie Falcon, she was going quit if Rod didn't start using mouthwash.

Jennifer had been right. This show was *vomiticious*. While I'd never had a problem before, I could now barely watch it being filmed. It lacked heart and soul. Just two fucking morons who in real life hated each other. Where was the romance?

The scene that was being shot was particularly challenging for Oral. They didn't call the character Oral for nothing. The private eye's favorite way of coming was in Daisy's mouth. But this scene called for him to come between her planet-sized tits in her heart-shaped, satin-sheeted bed. He had to take the globes in his hands and rub them against his foot-long cock. His "big gun," as he called it. Both stars were on their knees facing each other.

"You're hurting me, you fucking asshole!" screamed Daisy.

"Shut up, you fucking dyke!"

"Cut!" screamed Eddie. Neither line was in the script.

Finally, after ten takes, two breaks, and one walk off the set, Oral managed to explode between Daisy's chesticles. Cum poured down her torso as she arched her head back. The expression on her face was one of pure torture, but those watching the show would think she was in heaven.

"That's a wrap!" shouted Eddie with relief.

Thank God.

While the two actors stormed off the set, Eddie sauntered up to Vera and me. He cracked a smile and gave me a manly pat on the back. "Didn't expect to see you here, Blake. How's it going?"

"Great." *Get me the fuck out of here.*

"I'm really digging Vegas. The town's got so much talent."

"It depends on what you call talent," I snickered. Vera bit her lip to stifle a laugh.

"Hey, I'm about to have a meeting with a very talented director. I'd love for you to meet him. He's waiting in my office."

Against my better judgment, I agreed to join him.

Vera and I followed Eddie to his small office behind the set.

"Blake, I'd like you to meet—"

I could feel my face blaze with rage. My fists clenched so tightly my knuckles turned white. Gritting my teeth, I cut Eddie off.

"Get the fuck out of here. Or I'll kill you."

It was the fucking lowlife bastard. Don Springer. His face turned as fire-red as mine.

"Blake!" gasped Vera. Eddie remained speechless, his mouth agape.

"Vera, I'll explain later."

Springer leapt to his feet and stomped over to me. He was in my face. His fetid breath heated my cheeks. I couldn't bear sharing the air he breathed. It took all my willpower not to throw him out the door. And to keep my heart from beating out of my chest and exploding in his ugly face.

"Fuck you, Burns. You're going to pay big time." He spat at me and then stalked out of Eddie's office.

"I never want to see this man again anywhere on or near this set," I barked at Eddie while Vera grabbed a tissue from her purse and wiped the prick's spit off my chin.

Cowering, Eddie nodded. "Got it, boss."

"You call me if he comes back." Looping my arm through Vera's, I led her out of Eddie's office.

"Jesus. What the fuck was that all about? That was

Don Springer, right? The producer of *Wheel of Pain*."

I nodded as we headed back to her car. "That fucking bastard almost raped Jennifer on the set of *Wheel*." All the pain of that night seeped into my veins as I retold the horrific story.

"Oh my God!" gasped Vera, clasping her free hand to her mouth.

"If I hadn't gotten there when I did, God knows what he would have done to her. I cancelled the show and fired him on the spot."

"That was the right thing to do. The only thing to do."

"I'm sorry that I didn't tell you this earlier. I should have sent an e-mail out to everyone. With my flu last week, a lot of things went by the wayside."

"Blake, don't worry about it. Shit happens."

"I've made it so he never works in LA again."

"I have a lot of power in Vegas. I'm going to make sure that asshole never works in this town either."

I gave her a peck on the cheek. "Thanks, Vera. You're the best."

She broke into a smile. "Now, Superman, go save your relationship."

Chapter 11

Blake

At six in the evening, I caught my flight back to Los Angeles. Actually, I was flying into Burbank, a small retro airport located in the Valley not far from Dickwick's office. While LAX, LA's main airport, was much closer to my condo, I was unable to book my last minute flights from there. Not a big deal though I hated being in The Valley.

Sitting in first class, I was still reeling from my encounter with Springer. The fucking, fucking bastard. At least, he was now based in Las Vegas, far enough away from Jennifer. My need to protect her was fierce. It brought out a killer instinct I never knew I had. Heaven help the man who hurt her. Move over Superman, Batman, and Ironman. *Thatman,* my new alter ego, would cut his fucking balls off!

Knowing she was safe, my mind wandered. I wondered if she'd received my cactus plant. I was disappointed she hadn't e-mailed or texted me to thank me. Maybe she thought it was some kind of ruse. Or she didn't like cactus. Or she'd never gotten it. Nah. I could count on my mother's florist. Especially since she spent tens of thousands of dollars with him during the year—purchasing flowers for both our house and her many charitable galas.

I ordered a beer from the flight attendant. Savoring it, I pondered how I was going to prove that Jen's fiancé, Bradley Wick, DDS, was *vomiticious*. Totally not the right person for my tiger. Phase Three of *Operation Dickwick* was officially in effect. Hopefully, it would be the last.

Damn. Not one breakthrough idea. Almost as fast as we were up in the air, we were back down. The flight to Burbank was only forty-five minutes. We encountered no problems. Upon landing, I called for my car. I'd parked it with the valet. It was actually simpler than taking a cab, and plus, I got a free car wash.

The night was warm. Man, it was like we were having an endless summer while everyone in the rest of the country was freezing their asses off. My sparkling clean Porsche came around quickly. Pleased, I hopped into it and sped off.

Only minutes into the ride home, my stomach rumbled. I was starving. During Vera's whirlwind tour of our Vegas productions, I hadn't eaten a thing. I drove by one crap fast-food joint after another and then remembered a decent place where I could grab a bite to eat. The Smokehouse.

I hadn't been to the Smokehouse in Burbank in

ages. In fact, I'd only been here once before with my father. Around since the 1940s, it was very old school—big red leather booths, a meat-and-potatoes menu, and old-fashioned drinks. It was a haven for Hollywood old-timers. Especially those looking for a good fuck. It was no secret that hookers patrolled the bar looking for a well-paying lay.

For me, it was a sociological experience. Seated at my own dimly lit booth, I surveyed the gray hairs in garish polyester jackets looking to get some pussy. I wondered—would this be me in twenty years? I already had a couple of pre-mature grays, a gene I'd inherited from my silver-haired father. There was something pathetic about an older man trolling bars and looking for a hook-up. Maybe that's why my old man took me here—to show me how my life could turn out if I didn't settle down.

A waitress came by and asked for my order. She came with the territory—sexy but cheap-looking with a pile of brassy hair and boobs that could create a new bra size—double X. Strangely, she didn't turn me on, despite her seductive ways. I ordered another beer—a Coors, the only one on tap—and a cheeseburger with fries. My mind was focused solely on my dilemma—Jennifer McCoy. I was crazy about her. But I fucking didn't know how to handle it. Why couldn't she see her douchebag fiancé was all wrong for her? And why couldn't I prove it?

The chesty waitress came by quickly with my beer. Over a gulpful, I considered my next move. Maybe it was time to tell Jennifer I was the man she'd kissed in that game of Truth or Dare. Maybe, that would shake things up. *Or* screw things up. Frustrated, I slammed the mug back on the table and flipped open the copy *of The Hollywood Reporter* I'd brought along to entertain myself. Burying my eyes in the trade magazine, I caught up on the latest show biz goings-on. To my surprise, there was a small article about the cancellation of *Wheel of Pain*. News traveled fast in this town. Fucking Don Springer. Every muscle in my body tensed. *If I ever saw that fucking bastard again . . .*

My thought was cut short when a familiar scent assaulted me. I'm not talking barbecued beans. A powerful, cloying odor that nauseated me. Scrunching my face, I remembered where I'd encountered that smell. How could I forget? At the office of Bradley Wick, DDS. It was the *vomiticious* saccharine scent of his dental hygienist, Candace.

I glanced up from *The Reporter* and couldn't believe my eyes. Holy shit! There she was brushing past my table. All 36-24-36 of her packaged in the tightest, shortest mini skirt I'd ever seen and anchored in six-inch high heels. And she was dangling like a piece of jewelry on the arm of a man. Holy *fucking* shit! Bradley Wick, DDS. Dickwick. I took a quick gulp of my beer and almost gagged. He was out of his white lab coat and in his douchebag uniform—a poorly fitting navy blazer and two-inches too short khakis. D-cup Candace towered over him, but he wore her proudly as if she was a gold Rolex. I'm sure neither of them saw me. For sure, they would have stopped. They were too wrapped up with each other. But I had to be careful. Setting my mug back down on the table, I quickly lowered the baseball cap I was still wearing so they wouldn't recognize me and flipped on my shades. Move over Oral Covert, Private Dick. I was now Blake Burns, Secret Undercover Agent. The final phase of *Operation Dickwick* was now in full force. I was going to take him down.

I took another glug of the beer and watched stealthily as they slid side by side into a leather booth. Faster than I could say, "Busted," he was all over her, mouthing, fisting, and groping. What a fucking lowlife. Prickwick! Did Jennifer know her fucking fiancé was cheating behind her back? Boinking his sexy hygienist?

A light bulb lit up in my brain. I swear I could hear and see it ping the way they do in comic books. This had to be fate, meant to be. Jaime Zander's words flashed in my head. *Eliminate the competition.* Not wasting a second, I grabbed my cell phone and squatted below the table just so my eyes were above the surface. Aiming the phone at the amorous couple, I thumbed the camera icon, and adjusted the setting to "video." I tapped the screen and began recording Dickwick's little oral care session. My lips curled into a wicked smile. I was getting it all—their heated embrace, with lover boy's greedy little hands all over Candy-girl. Too bad, I was too far away to pick up any sound. But it was obvious; they were panting into each other's mouths, moaning, and groaning. It was the best adult entertainment I'd witnessed in years. Better than anything I'd ever seen on SIN-TV. Then the show ended. A waitress came by to take their order and they abruptly parted. Slightly embarrassed, Dickwick dabbed his slimy lips with a napkin. Hot lips, however, continued to nibble his neck. I stopped recording. I had everything I needed. Hastily, I dug my hands into my pocket for my wallet and slapped a hundred dollar bill onto the table. Though I'd never gotten my cheeseburger, this meal was worth every penny. In a flash, I was out of there, my phone secure in my hand.

Jennifer needed to know what a two-timing prick her future husband was. She was a nice girl. She deserved better. Someone who would fuck her brains out, not fuck with her brains. Someone who would be faithful and cherish her forever. Someone like me.

Seated in my Porsche that happened to be parked next to Bradley's Prius, I signed into one of my many bogus gmail accounts—charlespalmerthethird@gmail .com. The name sounded important and distinguished. I always got a quick response back from customer service whenever I used it.

To: jmccoy@sin.tv
From: charlespalmerthethird@gmail.com
Subject: Idea for a New TV Show

I continued to type away at the on-screen keyboard with my thumbs. There was only one thing they worked faster and better. Hint: It rhymed with "hit."

Dear Ms. McCoy:

Congratulations on your new job at SIN-TV. I am a producer of TV series, mostly reality-based. I thought the new show I've been developing would be a perfect fit for your network. I've attached a short video clip to give you a feeling for it. I'm tentatively calling it Dickwicks. I look forward to hearing back from you soon and to pitching you in the near future.

Sincerely,
Charles Palmer III
Executive Producer

I quickly proofed the letter—wanting badly to change "pitching you" to "fucking you"—and attached the footage to the e-mail. The internal laughter in my head was so loud it was deafening. They say seeing is believing. A fiendish smile spread across my face as I hit send. Success. It was now a waiting game until the conscientious Ms. McCoy opened her e-mail. I wished I could be there to see the expression on her face when she clicked on the attachment. Would her sweet mouth drop? Would she gasp? Would she shed tears? Would she respond to me? Of course, I wisely adjusted my setting to auto-reply: *Mr. Palmer is out of the office . . .*

I put my car in reverse and peeled out of the parking spot with a screech. I turned my satellite radio on to my favorite oldies channel. "Bad Boys," the theme song from that TV series *Cops*, blasted through the speakers as I sped up Barham Boulevard to the entrance of the 101.

I was a very bad boy. I had to admit. But I meant well. I was just looking out for the well-being of my employees. Their futures. In less than twenty-four hours, Jennifer McCoy would be newly single and available. I was sure of it. As I cruised along the freeway, a limerick popped into my head.

There once was a dentist named Bradley
Who was caught cheating one night badly.
His fiancée caught wind
That the fuckface had sinned
And that was the end of them sadly.

Tomorrow was going to be a great day at work. I couldn't wait.

Chapter 12

Jennifer

Burdened with shopping bags, I trudged into the living room of our small but cozy house. I'd just gotten back from Christmas shopping at The Grove. With its giant lit-up tree and fake snow, the popular, decked-out mall made the typically stressful experience fun. With Blake still in Vegas, I was able to sneak out of my office a little early. It turned out to be the perfect night to do my last-minute shopping and wrap up presents—Libby was once again doing evening focus groups, and Bradley was working late at his office. Earlier in the day, he'd called me and told me he was besieged with patients all wanting to see him before they went away for the holidays. He apologized for not getting in touch with me over the weekend. He was simply swamped with work and exhausted when he got home. His practice was obviously flourishing. More and more, he needed to work weekends and late hours.

I dumped the colorful bags on our coffee table and headed straight to the kitchen to make myself some hot chocolate. A mugful of the hot rich beverage along with some Christmas music was just what I needed to get into the mood for wrapping presents.

With "Jingle Bell Rock" playing in the background and the hot chocolate on the coffee table by the bags, I started wrapping the presents with the festive paper I'd bought. I was very pleased with my purchases. With the money I'd won in Vegas, I could afford to be a little indulgent. I'd gotten Libby a new pair of fuzzy slippers plus a DVD box set of the entire last season of *Bones;* her brother Chaz, a beautifully illustrated book on mid-century fashion, and Bradley, an expensive Italian designer silk tie—one he'd never spring for. It was going to be our first Christmas together as an engaged couple. He was flying home with me to celebrate the holidays with my parents. My mom and dad had met Bradley only once before—at a homecoming week-end—and they seemed to like him. That he came from a good family and had a good future ahead of him sat well with my overprotective parents.

I was also pleased with what I'd purchased for my parents—beautiful lambswool scarves from Ireland and each a book—for Mom, a California cuisine cookbook, and for Dad, a limited annotated Shakespeare collection. The only present I was unsure about was the one I'd bought for Blake. I mean, I hardly knew the man, and I wasn't even sure if it was appropriate to give your boss a gift. I doubted he was going to get anything for me, but I wanted to be on the safe side in case he did.

My first thought had been a cock warmer. I'd seen a goofy one with Rudolph the Red-Nosed Reindeer at a gift shop in the Farmer's Market adjacent to The Grove. I was tempted to buy it to send him a message. The jerk had e-mailed me that he was spending time with that bogus affiliate manager, but I suspected he'd stayed longer in Vegas to play with those blond bimbos. I was still smarting from his actions. In the end, my rationality triumphed over my emotions, and I decided the gag gift was inappropriate. And it was probably way too small for his big dick anyway. Instead, I settled on a snow globe that had a hammered gold Christmas ball—reminiscent of a matzo ball—inside it. I'd noticed he had a collection of these magical spheres on his office credenza and was sure I couldn't go wrong with it.

It took me an hour to wrap up all the gifts, label them, and finish them off with glittering bows. I placed all of them under the small Christmas tree Libby and I had purchased and decorated. The fresh pine scent filled the air and made Christmas feel alive.

I thought about calling Bradley—I felt bad that he had to work such late hours—but decided to check my e-mails first. Blake had a habit of sending me odd requests all night long—including some at ungodly hours. I wondered between fucking and working if the man ever slept. Instead of heading to my computer, I conveniently pulled out my cell phone from my nearby purse and went to my SIN-TV inbox. No e-mails from

Blake. I was partly relieved and partly disappointed. There was only one new e-mail. Sent earlier in the evening, it was from some producer named Charles Palmer III. Since being mentioned in *The Hollywood Reporter*, I'd received a lot of e-mails from producers and writers wanting to pitch me ideas for SIN-TV. I'd made it a policy to check and answer all of them. As Blake's father had said in my class at USC, "You never know where the next great idea will come from."

Sure enough, Mr. Palmer wanted to pitch me. His letter was to the point and included a short video presentation of the reality show he was developing. *Dickwicks.* I rolled my eyes. The name of his show was right up there with some of the other ideas that had come my way—*Balling for Dollars, Make Me Come*, and *Suck at It,* among them. With skepticism, I clicked open the attachment and hit play. All air left my lungs and my jaw dropped to the floor.

Oh. My. God. It was Bradley—all over his hygienist, Candace. My free hand flew to my mouth while the other one shook with the phone. My heart beat so hard I thought it would leap out of my chest. Tears poured down my face as sobs gathered at the base of my throat. How could he do this to me? How could I be so, so stupid? All those cancelled dates. All those late nights at work. Waves of nausea swept through me. About to puke, I leapt up, grabbed my bag, and stormed out the front door.

I swear, I don't know how accident-prone me managed not getting into a major accident. Tears blinded my vision as I drove down busy Ventura Boulevard to Bradley's condo in Sherman Oaks. He'd been able to buy it with the money his affluent parents had given him upon earning his dental degree.

Bradley's unit was located in a guard-gated community. I wiped my teary eyes with the sleeve of my sweater just before pulling up. The guard at the gate recognized me and smiled. "Good to see you, Miss McCoy. Happy Holidays."

Happy holidays were not in my foreseeable future. Holding it together as best I could, I wished him a Merry Christmas before another torrent of tears poured down my face. My voice quivered. "I have something to give to Bradley."

Oh yeah . . . I had something to give him all right. More precisely, to give *back* to him.

"Dr. Wick just got home. I'll let him know you're here."

A little panic button went off inside me. "Please don't let him know I'm here. I want to surprise him."

"Got it." The guard winked at me and clicked open the massive steel gate to let me into the complex.

The lights in Bradley's condo were on. The colorful, bright lights on the Christmas tree we'd decorated blinked in the front window. My heavy heart thudded as I jumped out of the car, and tears pooled in the back of my eyes. Though we'd decided not to live together before we got married, this is where we were going to spend the next years of our life once we did. Until we had kids.

The temperature had dropped. The now crisp December air ripped through me as I furiously pounded on the door. Shivering, I didn't have to wait long. Bradley came to the door quickly. He was still sporting the same blazer and trousers. The poisonous floral scent of Candace assaulted me and set my tangle of emotions into a tailspin. Wearing his preppy horn rim glasses in lieu of his contacts, my soon-to-be ex was surprised to see me.

"Hi, Jen. What are you doing here?" His voice was on edge. "Is everything okay?"

Fuck no. I whipped out my cell phone from my bag. I clicked onto the video and shoved the phone into his face.

"What were *you* doing here?" My voice shook with rage.

In tandem, his face blanched, his eyes rounded, and his mouth twitched. Then to my utter horror, he flashed his big toothy smile and chuckled. "Oh, it's nothing. Just a little Christmas smoo—"

I bitterly cut him off. "Don't bullshit me, Bradley.

You're fucking Candace. And you've been doing it for months." His eyes lowered. I'd called him on it. Victory fueled my rage. "When were you going to tell me? After we got married? Or maybe you expected me to drop in on one of your little late night work sessions?" *Fillings, my ass!*

Bradley chewed down on his bottom lip and shifted nervously in place. "Do you want to talk about it?"

A familiar voice sounded in the distance. "Braddie Waddie, what's going on?"

Candace. That's all it took. I did something I thought I'd never do in my life. With all my force, my free hand whipped across his face. I slapped him. Hard. The sound of the sting echoed in my ears.

Bradley winced with pain. Guess he could give it but couldn't take it. His hand flew to his face and rubbed the large red welt I'd left behind on his cheek-bone. I noticed for the first and last time how small his fingers were. Just like his roaming dick.

"Why'd you do that?" he moaned.

"For the same reason I'm going to do this," I shout-ed. Without wasting a second, I tore his engagement ring off from my finger and flung it at him. It bounced off a lens of his glasses and then landed with a ping somewhere on the front step.

"Bitch!" shrieked Bradley, his hand flying to his eyes. "You fucking broke my glasses!"

"And you fucking broke my heart, *Dickwick.*"

With that, I stormed back to the car. Scorching tears streamed down my ice-cold cheeks. My hands still shaking, I deleted the incriminating e-mail. And in my heart, I deleted Bradley. It was officially over for us.

When I got back to my house, Libby was home. Her Mini Cooper was parked in the driveway. I pulled up behind it and wearily made my way through the front door.

Libby was curled up on the couch drinking some wine. "Hi," she said brightly until she caught sight of my tear-stained face. "Sheesh. What the fuck is wrong? You look awful."

I'd cried so many tears I thought I had no more to shed. Wrong. A fresh batch sprung from my burning eyes. "I broke up with Bradley," I wailed.

"Oh my God." Libby jumped up from the couch and curled her arms around me. I wept on her shoulder. "Sit down and tell me everything," she said softly as she led me back to the couch.

Facing her, sitting cross-legged, I launched into the story of how I discovered Bradley was cheating on me with Candace. I paused occasionally to catch my breath or swipe away my tears.

Though never one to hold back, Libby listened intently and silently as I, blow by blow, told her what happened. Her hazel eyes blinked rapidly as she digested everything. Libby begged to see the footage, but I told her I'd deleted it. That I couldn't bear to watch it again.

When I got toward the end of my woeful tale, my bestie's freckled face lit up with surprise. "You seriously slapped his face?"

With a sniffle, I nodded. "And then I threw his ring at him and cracked his eyeglasses."

Libby burst into laughter and gave me hug. "Good for you. I never liked that dickwad. Trust me, it's meant to be he's out of your life. Just think if you'd married him."

"You're right," I conceded before taking a much needed sip of her red wine. The cheap Burgundy seeped through my veins and warmed me.

"What am I going to tell my parents? He was supposed to come home with me over the holidays. My mother was so excited. She even wanted to start planning the wedding."

Libby pensively knitted her brows together. "The truth. That you broke up with him. It wasn't working out. Less is best. They don't need to know all the details."

Libby was right—the truth was the only way to go. But I was going to wait till I got home to break the news to my overprotective parents. Why worry them sick now? I took another gulp of the comforting wine; it was beginning to dim the pain. My tears subsided.

"Lib, do you think it's weird that some strange producer sent me that footage?"

"Yeah, it's definitely a little random. But most likely, just a weird coincidence. You should take his pitch. Maybe he's some cute single guy."

"Shut. Up." Only Libby could make me laugh when all I wanted to do was cry.

"Sorry."

"I'm going to go call it a night."

"Maybe you should take a day off from work tomorrow. Sleep late and treat yourself to a massage."

While Libby's suggestion was so tempting, I didn't want to miss a day of work, having so recently started my job. I only hoped I could hold it together in front of Blake. The last thing I wanted was to let him see me blubbering like a child. It was bad enough he'd seen me make a drunken fool of myself in Vegas.

Fifteen minutes later, I was tucked in my bed. The footage of Bradley and Candace replayed in my head as if it were on a loop. Tears singed my eyes. We'd been together almost five years, and now in five minutes, it was over. Just like that.

In the morning on my way to work, I was going to drop off his Christmas present at the Salvation Army. Yes, I could return or exchange it, but I didn't want to touch or see anything that reminded me of Bradley Dickwick.

My tears succumbed to sleep.

Chapter 13

Blake

I got to my office super early; I couldn't wait to get there to see if my little ruse had worked. When I walked past her office, she wasn't at her desk yet. She was late. This could be a good sign or a bad one. Either she'd had a brutal breakup or major make-up sex with Dickwick. Shit. I'd never thought about the second possibility, and I didn't like it one bit.

Once settled in my office, I kicked up my legs on my desk and thumbed through the latest *Hollywood Reporter* to distract myself. On the last page dedicated to Hollywood happenings, there was a photo of me and Kitty-Kat or whatever the fuck her name was at Jaime Zander's art gallery opening. We were standing in front of *The Kiss,* the painting Jennifer adored. My pouty hook-up in her low-cut halter gown was sucking up to the camera. I looked rather solemn. The photo taken just after shithead Dickwick yanked Jennifer away from me. Hopefully, that wouldn't be happening again any time soon. My heart pulsed with anticipation. If *Operation Dickwick* was a success, Jennifer could be mine. All mine.

At the sound of a shuffle, I looked up and saw her. Dressed head to toe in black, she was back to wearing her glasses. But beneath the lenses, I could see her eyes were bloodshot and puffy. And she looked paler than usual. I had to refrain from smiling. All good signs. My eyes traveled down to her hands. Damn. She was holding a stack of books I'd asked her to option, making it impossible to see if she was wearing her ring. The tower of books extended from her waist to her chin. Definitely an overload. As she slumped toward me (another good sign, but maybe she was just weighted down by the books), I bid her good morning. When she lifted her chin to acknowledge me, the top book slipped off the pile. In an effort to save it, she panicked, and in an instant, all the books went flying to the floor. I heard her mumble "shit" under her breath as she fell to her knees to retrieve them. Mr. Chivalrous— yours truly—jumped up to help her, and in a nano second, I was squatting beside her. My eyes zeroed in on her left hand. It was shaking. But the ring was GONE! Mission accomplished!

"I'm sorry," she said in a small, trembling voice as she re-stacked the books. "Thanks for helping."

I was so close to her I could smell the sweet cherry vanilla scent of her hair and hear her heart thudding. Ahh! Music to my ears. The sound of a broken heart.

I added a couple of books to the heap. "You don't

seem your normal self today, Jennifer."

She sighed. I looked straight at her; she was so close I could taste her. Her eyes were watering.

"I'm fine," she replied as a tear spilled onto the cover of the top book. *Tangled.*

I lifted her glasses onto her head. The tears were freely falling down her cheeks. With the pads of my thumb, I brushed them away. Truthfully, I longed to kiss them away.

"You're not fine. Did something bad happen?"

"I broke up with my fiancé," she blurted. The forlorn look on her face got to me. I almost felt sorry for her. Sympathy was edging out my sense of victory.

"What happened?"

"He was cheating on me. With his hygienist."

"The blond one with the big tits?"

"Yeah, that one."

"That's awful. Do you want to take the day off?" *Hello, Mr. Nice Guy.*

Blinking back tears, she shook her head. "Thanks, Blake, but no. I think work will keep my mind off things. And I've got a lot on my plate. I want to review the focus group findings with Libby and start optioning these erotic romances. Plus, there's the staff meeting."

She stacked the last book on the pile and awkwardly tried to gather up the bundle. "Let me help you." I offered. My fingers brushed against hers as I grabbed the top half of the stack and stood up. She followed suit with the rest of the books and thanked me again.

"Where would you like the books?" she sniffled, her pools of green burning a hole right through me.

"On my desk would be just fine." I led the way, and we set the two piles side by side next to my computer. She caught sight of the photo in *The Hollywood Reporter,* and her breath hitched in her throat. She bit down on her lip and her eyelids fluttered.

"Are you sure you're going to be okay?" I asked.

She nodded, still staring at the photo. "I think about that night a lot."

"I do too." Of how much I wanted her in my arms and her lips back on mine. Now that dream could be a reality. Dickwick was out of her life.

She pivoted on her heel. "Well, I'd better get back to my office. I want to prepare for the staff meeting. Oh, and I almost forgot. Thank you for that cactus plant. I got it this morning."

"Just a little token of my appreciation." *Of my affection.* We exchanged small smiles.

As I headed to my chair and she to the door, she spun around and asked me a question.

"Mr. Burns, one last thing. Do you know a producer by the name of Charles Palmer III?"

I stopped dead in my tracks and swallowed hard. "Very well. But he's very difficult to connect with. Let me know if you hook up with him. I'd love to meet him."

Another small smile curled up on her sweet lips. "I will. See you in a bit at the staff meeting."

"Later," I retorted and she disappeared.

Right now, I had to figure out my next move with Ms. Jennifer McCoy.

Back in my chair, I stared blankly at the photo in *The Hollywood Reporter*. No more Kitty, Kirstie, Kristie, or Keira. There was only one girl for me. Only one girl I longed to kiss. But how was I going to make her mine? Then like a meteorite, an idea crashed into my brain. I speed-dialed my best bud. Jaime Zander.

Chapter 14

Jennifer

The next couple of days were pure hell. While the mood in the office was festive because of the holidays, I was miserable.

The last thing I wanted to do was go to the company-wide Conquest Broadcasting Christmas Ball. I was still reeling from the aftershock of my breakup with Bradley. Most of my single co-workers were bringing dates. All I had to bring was a broken heart. Worst of all, the party was being held at Greystone Manor, the club where I'd celebrated my short-lived engagement just weeks ago. Hiding in my bed, I threw the covers over my head. From beneath them, I heard my door crack open and footsteps approaching. Libby.

"Come on, girlfriend. Get your ass out of bed and get ready."

"Do I have to go?" I groaned, one eye peeking out from the duvet.

"The Christmas party will be good for you; you've got to get over being a victim." Dressed in a black velvet mini-dress, Libby admired herself in my mirrored armoire as she clipped some sparkling earrings onto her lobes. "It was a blast last year. Mel Weiner from Finance got drunk and fucked a chair. They had to carry him out."

Big whoop. Seeing some fifty-old horny man getting off on an inanimate object was not my idea of fun. I had an excuse.

"I have nothing to wear." Over the past week, I'd had neither the time nor inclination to shop for a new dress. And I'd forgotten to pick up Chaz's perfect little black dress from the dry cleaner. While I had several gowns that I'd worn to Bradley's—scratch that, Dickwick's—dentist events hanging in my closet, I truthfully wanted to burn them. In fact, maybe that's what I would do tonight. Yuletide party for one.

"Your fairy godmother has arrived." At the sound of a familiar cheery, singsong voice, I bolted upright to a sitting position and then hopped out of bed. It was Chaz, Libby's twin brother, dressed in outrageous black leather shorts, a red velvet blazer, and sparkling red high tops. Dangling from his hands were two monstrous Merry Christmas shopping bags with naked Santas dancing on them. He pranced into my room.

"What's Chaz doing here?" I asked Libby.

"He's *our* date for the Xmas party. No party is a party without Chaz. Last year, he got everyone to do the 'Hokey Pokey.'" She broke into the juvenile song and dance. "You put you both boobs in. You put your both boobs out. You put your both boobs in, and you shake them all about," she belted out in her husky off-key voice. Without reserve, she shimmied her C-cup chest, and then we all turned ourselves around as she continued to croon.

Despite my doom and gloom mood, I burst into much needed laughter.

"My lovelies, just consider yourself lucky." Chaz beamed. "And here are your Christmas presents from yours truly." He handed us each a bag.

Libby squeed as she removed the contents of hers. "Oh, bro, it's fabulous! I'm going to change!"

She held up the dress in front of her. It was one sexy number. A bandage-like red sequined strapless dress—custom-made for her curvy little body and wild vermilion hair.

Libby darted out of the bedroom with the dress draped over her arm.

"What are you waiting for, Jenny-Poo?" asked Chaz.

I frowned. "I don't want to go."

"Stop it. Nonsense. You're going as my date. And that's that. And you're going to be the belle of the ball. Now, take a look-see at what's inside the bag."

Reluctantly, I reached inside the bag. Under layers of sparkly red tissue paper, a combination of silk, tulle, and sequins grazed my fingers. I removed the dress, laid it on the bed, and gawked. It was dazzling. A strapless emerald green confection with a pouf of glittering layers of tulle that reminded me of the sprigs of an evergreen tree. A sparkling tulle wrap accompanied the dress along with a pair of matching green satin pumps.

"Oh my God! It's beautiful." There was no doubt in my mind that one day Chaz would be right up there with Marc Jacobs and Michael Kors.

With a wide Cheshire cat grin, Chaz gleefully clapped his fingertips together. "And it's going to be even more beautiful on you. Now, my Cinderella, get ready before my Jeep transforms into a pumpkin." He sashayed out of the bedroom.

I had no choice. I was going to the Christmas party. Libby was probably right. It would be good for me. To get out of my misery. To meet new people with the company. And to show my boss that I was a team player. As I stepped into the green dress, an unsettling thought crossed my head—would Blake be there with a date? I shivered. Without a doubt. With one of his blond bimbos.

All dressed up, I suppressed the disquieting thought and took a look at myself in my armoire mirror. I was actually startled. With the way I'd been looking and feeling over the last few days, I seriously didn't think I could look this good. The dress fit me perfectly with the last layer of tulle grazing my mid thighs. The six-inch heels made my long legs look impossibly longer. With my contacts on, my eyes sparkled green—almost the same shade as the dress. My thick hair was gathered into a high ponytail, and on my ears, two cubic zirconia studs glittered like diamonds. I wrapped the tulle stole around my shoulders. I gave myself a little smile and my reflection smiled back. Cinderella was ready for the ball.

Chapter 15

Jennifer

The Conquest Broadcasting Christmas Ball was already in full swing by the time Libby, Chaz, and I got there. Techno music was blasting and the vast club was packed. It was hard to believe this many people worked for Conquest Broadcasting. In addition to the strobing disco balls, strings of colorful Christmas ornaments and glistening gold stars hung from the ceiling. The effect was dazzling. My eyes darted around the two-level nightclub. People were eating, drinking, socializing, and dancing. I recognized a few of my co-workers from SIN-TV. Even stoic Mrs. Cho was here. She looked fabulous in a gold lamé dress and was a dancing up a storm with an Asian man who must be her husband. Blake Burns, however, was nowhere in sight.

"Let's go to the bar and get something to drink," insisted party animal Libby.

"I'll meet you there," replied Chaz. "I'm going to the buffet for a bite to eat." He sashayed away leaving me alone with Libby.

Libby grabbed me by the elbow. "Come on. Let's

go. Have a drink ticket ready."

The company had issued each employee three drink tickets, a necessary precaution to prevent people from overdrinking. Thinking back to my embarrassing chocolatini spree in Vegas, that was something I was definitely not going to do.

We wove through the crowd. The bar was packed three people deep.

"This is crazy," grumbled Libby who wasn't known for her patience. "I'm gonna check out the buffet and come back later."

"I'm going to stick it out." I really needed a drink. Being back at the club where I'd celebrated my engagement and kissed that beautiful stranger was making my stomach bubble with nerves. Moreover, the crowd was making me feel claustrophobic.

I inched closer to the bar. But some rude, aggressive types cut in front of me. From behind me, I heard a warm, familiar voice.

"Well, hello, Jennifer. Are you enjoying your first Conquest Christmas Ball?"

I spun around. It was Blake's father—Saul Bernstein, the head of Conquest Broadcasting. He was wearing an elegant pewter-gray suit and a bright red silk tie. Two recognizable women flanked him. On one side: his stunning wife, Helen, dressed to the nines in an elegant chartreuse silk sheath and a complement of sparkling diamonds, and her platinum hair swept up. On the other side: Blake's octogenerian grandma, Muriel, in a silver-beaded dress that matched the color of her hair.

I plastered a smile on my face. "Yes, Mr. Bernstein, it's a lot of fun." *I just want to go home and crawl into bed.*

"You look absolutely lovely, my dear," breathed Mrs. Bernstein.

"Thank you. You do too." She smiled graciously and thanked me for the compliment.

"Bubala, have you seen *Blakela?"* chimed in Grandma.

The mention of his name made my stomach turn and my heartbeat quicken.

"No," I stuttered.

"Vhat are you? Blind? He's standing right over there."

My eyes followed her sweeping hand gesture. My heart skipped a beat. There he was leaning against a doorway close to the table where I had kissed *that* man. He looked absolutely devastating—clad in a forest green velvet smoking jacket over a crisp white dress shirt and black bowtie, and his hair slicked back. His eyes connected with mine. Every nerve ending in my body flickered. My legs turned to jelly. And then, he signaled with his index finger for me to come over to him. His eyes burned a hole through me from across the room.

"Excuse me," I stammered, my heart pitter-pattering.

"Go *kibbitz* with him," I heard Blake's grandmother shout out as I headed his way. With legs of Jell-O, I don't know how I made it through the dense crowd without tripping in my six-inch heels. Someone was looking out for me.

I stopped in front of him. Still seductively perched against the doorway, he smiled that cocky dimpled smile. My breath hitched in my throat, and my heart thudded so loudly in my chest I could hear it. And I'm sure he could hear it too.

"Hi," I managed.

"Hi, tiger," he breathed back. His gaze traveled from my head to my toes and then his smoldering eyes looked directly into mine. "You look beautiful."

"Thanks," I squeaked. One-word answers with one syllable were all I could muster.

"Do you know where we're standing?"

"No." I swore I wasn't even sure where I was.

"Under the mistletoe."

"Oh." I gazed up and saw a small leafy branch with red berries dangling from the doorframe.

"Do you know what means?"

"No," I murmured.

His piercing blue eyes searched mine. We were a palm's width apart, so close I could feel his heated breath on my face. Sensations coursed through me I had no right feeling. Heart palps. Shortness of breath. And hot tingles all over. And I couldn't blame it on the alcohol because I hadn't had a drop to drink. His velvety virile voice sounded again in my ear.

"Jennifer, it means I have to kiss you," he said softly, his eyes never leaving mine. "It's good luck."

"Oh."

My vocabulary was down to one word. I swallowed a gulp of air. He was having an unnerving effect on me. I wanted his lips on mine in a sinful way. Nibbling, gnawing, biting. Parting them with his tongue. Sucking. *Jennifer, get a grip. He's your boss!*

"Bla—"

Before I could finish saying his name, his mouth crashed onto mine, and his hand fisted my ponytail, yanking back my head.

Oh. My. God. From the very second his lush lips latched onto mine, there was something familiar about him. Something déjà vu. The way he gripped my ponytail and wrapped it around his hand and pulled back my head. The delicious pain mixing with the delicious pleasure. The fierceness of the kiss. The way it made my head spin out of control. Oh. My. God. Could it be? Could it be *him?* And then when his tongue parted my lips and entwined with mine, there was little doubt in my mind. The taste of champagne on his palette. The way his tongue tangoed with mine. The moans, the groans. Oh God! It *was* him! *That* man I'd kissed at my engagement party. Holy, holy, holy fuck! I gripped his collar as I did the first time we'd kissed, this time because I thought I might faint if I didn't cling to him.

The world around me disappeared. Muted. I could vaguely hear Mariah Carey singing in the background, "All I Want for Christmas is You." A chorus of moans and groans accompanied the song as his tongue tangled with mine in a hot sensual dance. He tugged harder on my ponytail, tightening his grip, until I was throbbing at the roots, desperate for more.

My heart racing, my breathing harsh, I finally tore away. "You're *that* man," I gasped, one hand flying to my wide-open mouth. My eyes forgot to blink as a whirling dervish of emotions whished around in my head.

Excitement.

Shock.

Confusion.

Desire.

"Yeah, tiger. I'm *that* man."

My eyes met his in a flurry of flutters. "How do I know for sure?"

A saucy smile curled on his lips. "You were wearing a peach silk dress, those fake diamonds in your ears, and silver shoes with little bows. And there was a SpongeBob Band-Aid on your knee."

I gasped. He'd recited everything I was wearing that

night, right down to the Band-Aid on my razor nick.

"Convinced?"

I nodded feverishly as he trailed kisses up my neck. Holy, holy fucking shit! Blake Burns, my boss, was *that* man! That beautiful stranger I'd kissed blindfolded in a game of Truth or Dare. Right here in this club. Almost in this exact same spot.

"Good. Let's get of here," he breathed into my ear. "I think you need to be more than kissed."

Beneath my dress, all air escaped my lungs. He lowered my hand from my face and lifted it to his lips. Tenderly, he kissed the back of my palm. Clasping the hand he'd just kissed, he led me through the sardine-packed crowd. Dazed, I followed him, trying hard not to trip on my six-inch heels and hoping my knees wouldn't buckle. I focused on the warmth of his hand, gripping mine. People were too busy socializing to notice our escape. Or his hand entwined with mine.

"Where are we going?" I mumbled under my shaky breath.

"Somewhere private."

A hot throbbing wet mess, I let him lead the way.

Five minutes later, we were standing face-to-face in a remote part of the club, far away from the party, in a dimly lit intimate room that resembled a bedroom. It was minimally furnished in shades of gray with a built-in big screen TV, a sleek credenza bearing an orchid plant, and a massive bed draped in satin sheets. The walls were upholstered except for the one facing the bed, which was mirrored. Catty-corner to it, was a door that could either be a closet or a connection to another room.

My heart raced as my eyes stayed fixed on the inviting bed. "What is this place?"

"A private room I keep here," he whispered as he walked me backward toward a wall until I was plastered against the upholstery. His hips pressed against mine, and his palms against the padding, bracketing my head. His warm lips gnawed at my neck, my shoulders, my chest, and then made their way back to my hungry mouth. Oh those delicious lips! He deepened the kiss as his erection dug into my belly.

Reality to brain. Come in, please. My breaths morphed into pants; my temperature soared. I was making out with my boss, Blake Burns, in what must be his fuck pad. *That* man whose lips had consumed mine on the night of my engagement party. Yes, *that* man! This was all so wrong. Yet so right. So unreal but really happening. I should have been flipping out and running for the door, but my mind was in meltdown and my legs in cement. I forced reason into my brain.

"I should go." I could barely get the words out.

He nibbled my ears. There must have been a string attached to my pussy because hot tingles danced all around it. And then one word: "No."

"You're my boss," I gasped.

"Yes, and I'm ordering you to stay. You want this as much as I do. Now, come to Santa, baby."

Before I could say another word, his lips returned to my mouth. His warm, long-fingered hands cradled my face as his tongue nudged my lips to part. Back inside my mouth, it twirled and whirled with mine, doing that dance. I was melting into him. Unable to resist. He was right. I did want this. Maybe even more than he did.

I clenched my eyes shut as our mouths became one, clinging hotly together. A hand reached behind me, squeezing into the narrow space between my back and the wall. The hiss of the zipper inching down my dress filled my ears. And then I felt two supple hands slide the sparkly confection off me. In a breath, my bare breasts were rubbing against his soft velvet jacket. My sensitive nipples ached with want. I opened my eyes a slit's worth as he read my mind.

With tiny gasping breaths, I watched as he tweaked my buds between his thumbs and index fingers. His eyes, now hooded, gazed down at them. A delicious smile curled on his lips.

"Oh, baby, they're even pinker and more perfect than I imagined."

A buzzing sensation coursed through me as my hazy brain digested his words. He'd called me "baby" again and insinuated that he'd fantasized about me. Me, Calamity Jen!

As he played with my nipples and sucked my lips, a

new ache crescendoed between my legs. I wanted him. I fucking wanted him. A want like I'd never experienced before. Every nerve in my body was sparking and my heart was on fire.

And then I jolted. A hand reached down into my lace bikinis and found its way to the molten folds between my thighs. After stroking them, his skilled fingers glommed onto my clit and circled it. Flutters of pleasures met his touch. I let out a moan. Or was it a groan? Either way, ecstasy powered it.

"Jesus." he said, his voice a deep breathy whisper. "You're so fucking wet for me, you bad girl."

No one had ever called me "bad" before. I'd always been a good girl through and through. I came from a good family, did good things, had good friends, went to a good college, got a good job . . . and had been engaged to a good guy. So I'd thought.

Fuck. I want to be bad, I thought as I let him slide my undies down my legs, inch by sweet inch. That classic Christmas song, "Santa Claus is Comin' to Town" filtered into the room through hidden speakers. He rewarded the good; punished the bad. Honestly, who gave a fuck what *that* Santa thought. *My* secret Santa was showering me with wonderful surprises.

My panties hung low at my feet with my dress.

"Step out of them," he purred in my ears. One foot after another, I did as bid. Except for my heels, I was totally naked and wrapped in his strong arms.

"Good girl." Okay, so now I was good. I was so delirious with rapture, I didn't know the difference between good and bad. And I didn't give a damn.

With one hand, he worked his slacks, freeing his cock.

I glanced down and gasped. His erection was even bigger than I remembered, and it was pointed my way. With eyes wide, I watched as he slipped his hand into one of his slacks pockets and pulled out a small foil package. A condom. His ripped it open with his teeth. The hissing sound sent another rush of moisture to my core.

"Put this on me," he commanded.

Inch by thick inch, I rolled the sheath up his monstrous shaft. The heat of it singed my fingertips.

With a satisfied smirk, he lifted me up against the upholstered wall and growled, "Now wrap your arms and legs around me."

He was my boss. Still in my stilettos, I did as he asked. I held my breath as he nudged the crown of his hot cock into my center. We were perfectly lined up. Slowly, he slid it inside me, stretching me, until he filled me to the hilt. My fingernails dug into the fabric of his jacket, and I winced with sweet pain. Holy shit! I thought he was going to split me open.

"Am I hurting you?"

"No," I said as my muscles relaxed and got used to his size.

"Christ, tiger, you're so tight and wet. I want to fuck you so badly." His eyes burned into mine. "I'm going to show you what it's like to be fucked and by a man who knows how."

I absorbed his words, absorbed his girth. He was so different from Bradley. So hot, so full, so big. So divine! Gripping my bottom, he began to pound into me. I clung to his biceps and tugged at his hair, unable to suppress my moans. My hips rocked with his. I knew I should be thinking about the consequences of my actions, but any logical thought at the moment was impossible.

"Do you like this?" he breathed.

"Yes." *Oh yes!*

Good girl, bad girl. It no longer mattered. With each forceful thrust, he was pushing me over the edge. Creating exquisite sensations inside me I'd never experienced. A pressure, so electrifying, so intense I was seeing stars of Bethlehem.

"Do you want to come?"

"Yes. Oh please, yes!" *Yes, yes, YES!* I fisted the lapels of his velvet blazer.

He pumped harder, faster, rubbing against my clit with each unrelenting stroke. His breaths came in pants. My own pants gave way to whimpers. I was desperately craving a release.

"Don't hold back," he growled between gritted teeth. "I want to hear you roar, tiger. The room is soundproof."

All it took was a squeeze of my clit. "Come for Santa," he breathed into my mouth.

With a roar of his name so loud it echoed, I imploded. Tears leaked from my eyes as fierce waves of ecstasy swept through my body. A moment later, he let out his own primal roar. His hot pulsing cock exploded inside me, soaking me with his release, as I shuddered around him.

Through the speakers, "Have Yourself a Merry Little Christmas" piped into the chamber. Spent, Blake rested his glistening sweat-laced forehead against mine as I clung to him. His breathing calmed. I was still shuddering and sobbing softly.

"Merry Christmas, tiger," Blake whispered in my ear.

"Merry Christmas."

Christmas had come early.

Chapter 16

Blake

Christ. I'd wanted to kiss her ever since the first time my lips touched down on hers. Taste her mouth in mine. Bite her lips, dance with her tongue. It had been weeks of torture and frustration. I'd jerked myself off so many times I had calluses.

It was different this time. Better. So much better, if better was possible. I was no longer a blind accident. I could tell. She wanted me as much as I wanted her.

She tasted so fucking good. I could feel her heartbeat in her mouth and her pulse in her neck as I trailed kisses down the slender length. The way she groped at my clothing and my hair bordered on savage. I was as ruthless as she was. We couldn't get enough of each other.

I couldn't stop tongue-fucking her mouth. Even before I saw those tender tits exposed in their full glory for the first time, I needed more. I had to have all of her. Have all of me inside her. When my fingers reached down to her clit, I knew she was ready. She was so fucking hot and wet. With the office Christmas party raging outside and Christmas carols drifting inside, I disrobed her and took her against the wall.

I'll never forget the expression on her face when she saw my whopper cock. Her eyes glittered like two green gumdrops and her rosebud lips quivered. Yeah, she'd seen it once before—accidentally at my parents' Shabbat dinner. But only from a distance. A funny thought crossed my mind. Mr. Burns, as I sometimes affectionately called my dick, was ready for his close-up. Oh was he! A good thing I'd packed him a debut outfit. A top-of-the-line custom-sized condom.

Her fingers trembled as she inched it up me. I thought my thick, hard-as-nails cock might bust the delicate sheath. But she got it up without a tear. Without wasting a second, I put the broad tip to her pussy, and in a hot breath, I penetrated her.

Jesus Christ. She was tight. So fucking tight. Taking it slow, I slid my cock deep inside her. My eyes stayed glued on her face. Clenching her eyes, she chewed down on her lip and squeaked out a groan. Fuck. I was ripping her apart. And then, her muscles relaxed. I glided easily inside her, her drenched walls making it almost effortless. I began to pound her and quickly got into a rhythm. She was sexual and responsive. With breathy moans and groans, she met my thrusts, and as our pace picked up, I gripped her sweet, smooth ass. Sweat laced her svelte body, and an intoxicating scent—a delicious blend of sex and cherry vanilla—

filled the air we breathed. I inhaled her like cocaine. She was a drug I couldn't get enough of, a drug that made me high with lust and desire. I'd never been so turned on.

Her breathing became ragged. I could feel her falling apart at the seams. I knew she was close to coming, and she confirmed it with one gasping word: "Yes." Fuck, I loved that word. With one final deep thrust and a pinch of her clit, I brought her to her climax. As my tiger roared out my name, I watched her chest flush, her eyes gush tears, and her body shudder. It was the most beautiful thing I'd ever seen. And then I juddered in her sea of waves with the most explosive orgasm I'd ever had in my life. To my surprise, I could go again. And wanted to madly.

Before I could make another move, she broke free of me. Where the hell was she going? I'd just begun. My eyes stayed fixed on her as she crouched down to pick up her sparkly green dress sprawled by my feet. Standing up, she stepped into it and shimmied it up her perfect little body. I felt bereft as I watched her preened pussy and her sweet breasts with their dainty puckered nipples disappear behind the fabric. She silently struggled with the back zipper.

I came to the rescue. But before I inched up the zipper, I studied her back. I loved everything about it— her creamy porcelain skin, her sculpted shoulder blades, the gentle slope of her spinal cord, and above all, those two little dimples at her tailbone. I longed to dip my tongue into those sexy indents after trailing kisses down every step of her spine and then tear off her dress. My still semi-erect cock hardened at the thought of having her naked in my arms again. And fucking her in this position, from the back, until she roared one more time with ecstasy. I'd never had to beg for sex; I didn't even know how. All I knew how to do was fuck girls into submission and usually *they* begged for it.

She never got the chance to slip on her panties. Unable to control myself, I lived out my fantasy and laved my tongue down her spine. Her bony discs made me feel like I was skiing over mogels. It was as thrilling as an extreme sport. Halfway down, my cock jumped up. Fuck. I was getting another erotic high.

"Please, Blake," she moaned, flexing her hips and arching her head back. The tip of her ponytail tickled my throat.

"Please what?" I growled against her neck.

"Please take me."

Home? Not a chance in hell.

"All of me," she breathed out.

Way to go, Blakemeister! I didn't expect her to make it so easy—to beg for me. In an instant, I shoved down her dress and rubbed my cock against her backside until it was as hard as it needed to be. I spread her legs, and then gripping her hips, I slid my rigid length between them. She moaned with blissful pleasure as the tip of my cock powered back into her. A groan escaped my throat. Man, she was still soaking wet and so fucking hot. Wrapping one arm around her slender waist and the hand of the other around a tender breast, I hammered her. Finding my rhythm, her hips rocked back and forth with mine with every deep, mighty thrust. I could feel her heat radiating. I moved the hand kneading her exquisite tit to her dripping wet pussy. My fingers caressed the slick, silky folds and then made their way to her swollen clit. They pressed hard against it, running circles around it.

"Oh God. Oh God. Oh God," she repeatedly cried out. Whimpers quickly replaced words.

"Oh, baby, you feel so fucking good; so tight and warm," I breathed in her ear. My mouth stayed there, showering her neck with hot kisses. God, she tasted good. So, so good.

"Oh, Blake!" she moaned.

I loved when she said my name. "Are you close to coming again?"

"So close," she panted out.

I rubbed her clit harder and pounded into her force-fully. The sound of my flesh slapping against hers joined her chorus of harsh breaths and whimpers.

"So, so, close." Her rasp was just above a whisper. A desperate whisper.

On the next thrust, she broke loose once more, com-ing around me in spades of screams and spasms. Her body went limp, and I held her firmly so she wouldn't crumple as my own mind-blowing climax met hers with another powerful thrust. We stayed locked in this position as we rode our orgasms out.

"Oh, tiger, that was fucking amazing," I breathed into her ear while caressing her soaking wet pussy. Her folds still hypersensitive to my touch, I felt her shudder yet again against me.

Only one word tumbled out of her mouth. "More."

After another round of mind-blowing sex—this time on the floor—we were spent. Both of us now naked to the bone, we sat against a padded wall catching our breaths. Jen's ponytail had come loose. Her dark shoulder-length waves cascaded over my green velvet jacket. I'd placed it over her shoulders like a cape. Her knees were curled up with her arms folded around them. There was something so sexy about seeing her in this position and wrapped up in my way too big jacket.

Victory. My cock was one happy camper. And so was I. Dickwick was gone and now she was mine. I slung an arm around her as she rested her chin on her knees. God, she was adorable. My invincible cock stirred. Could I take her one more time? Make her a record?

The luxurious bed in my fuck pad was tempting, but

she didn't belong there. It was where I'd fucked all my hook-ups and watched them come in the mirror across from it. Jennifer was not a hook-up. She was something more. Someone special. The first woman I wanted to bring home. To fuck in my real bed, hold in my arms, and wake up to in the morning. A sharp pang of remorse stabbed at me. I squeezed my eyes. Shit. I shouldn't have fucked her here. Someone special deserved somewhere special.

I nuzzled her neck and then whispered in her ear, "Come on, beautiful. Let's get out of here. Come home with me." In my heart, I hoped it wasn't too late to make amends.

She bit down on her lip and shook her head. Her expression went from tortured ecstasy to a mixture of confusion and despair. Tears spilled from her eyes.

With my other hand, I tilted up her chin. "What's the matter, tiger?"

She turned and faced me. Her pained eyes searched mine. Yup. It was too late. I'd fucked up. My heart drummed as her sweet lips parted.

"This is all wrong. You're my boss."

"So what?" This was not the response I expected from her.

"Blake, it's just a onetime thing. A fluke. I'm vulnerable. You got me on the rebound."

"What are you trying to say?" My voice was a desperate rasp.

"Let's forget this ever happened."

"Tiger, how can you say that?"

"I just got out of one of bad relationship. I don't need to start another—especially with my boss."

"It doesn't have to be a relationship. We can just be discreet fuck buddies." My voice sunk with desperation. Hers rose with rage.

"Oh? You mean, I could be one of your hook-ups like Kitty-Kat or whatever her name is? I. Don't. Think. So." She paused and then her voice turned to ice. "Blake, I need to get dressed."

Fuck. Why did I say that? How could I be so goddamn stupid? So goddamn desperate? "Jennifer, I didn't mean it that way. Honestly."

"My father says words can't be taken back. So, if you'll please excuse me, I'd like to leave."

I rested my chin on the top of her head and held her firmly. "Don't go," I begged. "Please don't go."

"Blake, please. I need to get dressed and go home."

Squirming, she broke free of me and shrugged off my jacket. She slid across the padded wall and stood up. Hurriedly, she threw on her dress. She didn't even bother with her panties.

My emotions in a jumble, I leapt to my feet. "Fine. Then I'll take you home." Maybe I could get her into *her* bed. It didn't have to be mine. I needed to prove to her she was more than a casual lay. I gripped her arm, holding her back.

She jerked away. Tears swam down her cheeks. "Mr. Burns, please. Don't touch me. I've made up my mind." Before I could say another word, she fled. The door to my fuck pad slammed shut behind her.

Defeated, I slumped down against the wall. Shit-balls. I wasn't expecting this. I was positive with Dickwick out of her life, she'd be all mine. Especially after learning I was *that* man she'd kissed in that game of Truth or Dare. I'd had the whole night planned out, from the mistletoe to the morning after. Grandma had even helped. I buried my head between my knees.

Jesus. How could I have been so wrong? She wasn't ready for another relationship. And I'd said some stupid, stupid things. Mr. Hook-Up had no idea how to handle a relationship. I was a player. I left women; they never left me. Until now.

Jennifer McCoy was gone with the wind. Maybe I'd shown her what it was like to be kissed—and fucked—by someone who knew how, but that wasn't enough. I sure hadn't lined up my cherries. I'd made a total mess of tonight. I reached for her panties—a souvenir of our encounter—and sniffed them. A glimmer of hope lifted me out of my misery. After all, tomorrow was another day.

Chapter 17

Jennifer

My alarm clock went off at exactly six fifteen. There was actually no need to set it. I didn't sleep a wink. How could I? I kept replaying what had happened at the office Christmas party. My mind was a whirlwind of chaos. Caused by two opposing forces—lust and remorse.

Holy, holy fuck. It was all too much. All too unbelievable. Blake Burns was *that* man I'd kissed at my engagement dinner. My boss! *That* man whose kiss I couldn't forget. And now I'd fucked him. Not once. Not twice. But three times. And after the first time, I'd begged for it and even torn off his clothes.

Blake had fucked my brains out. Fucked me senseless. I'd never had an orgasm from intercourse before, let alone three in a row, each one sending me over the edge. Blake Burns had brought me to a place I'd never been. And all through my sleepless night, I'd relived the moments of our mind-blowing sex. Over and over. Coming against the wall, my legs wrapped around him. Coming in his arms, taking me from behind. Coming on my knees, falling with him to the floor. Our hands, our mouths, our tongues everywhere. I couldn't get enough of his magnificent body. Or his magnificent cock.

As my breathing wound down after the third time, a soupçon of sense had crept back into my head. What I'd done was wrong. But what he'd done was more wrong. He'd taken advantage of me in my vulnerable state. And I'd succumbed. Why? Because he was beautiful? Because his kiss sent me orbiting? Because he'd given me one mind-blowing orgasm after another? Because he was *that* man I'd dreamt about incessantly ever since our first passionate kiss?

A tangle of emotions swirled around in my head. The bottom line: I couldn't have a relationship with my boss. I had a career at stake. It had to end before it began. And then he'd made it so easy for me. How could I be so blind? He wanted me to be just another one of his hook-ups. A convenient fuck with no strings attached. Reality had thrown an axe at me, but I didn't expect my heart to bleed.

Now, I had to face him. My boss. Thank God, it was the last day of work before my Christmas break. Tomorrow, I was flying home to spend the holidays with my parents. Though I dreaded breaking the news to them that I'd broken up with Bradley, who was supposed to have flown home with me, I looked forward to getting away. I needed time away from Los Angeles and, above all from Blake, to clear my head.

Hopefully, by the time I got back, what'd happened last night would be just a vague memory. Something I could call a moment of weakness. A stupid, regrettable mistake.

I dragged myself out of bed, showered, and got dressed. Every ordinary task was an effort. It wasn't easy concentrating. I was preoccupied with how to deal with my boss. And I was throbbing in the place where his cock, his hands, and his mouth had been. I was an emotional and physical wreck.

Libby was already in the kitchen, and coffee was made. I helped myself to a mugful. I needed a caffeine fix desperately.

"Where did you disappear to last night?" she asked. She was seated at the counter, sipping her coffee over the *LA Times.*

"Restroom," I lied, after taking a sip of the steamy brew. I wasn't ready to tell Libby about what had happened with Blake last night. I was too hurt and confused.

Ms. Inquisitive's rust-colored brows furrowed. "Why so long?"

"I must have eaten something bad or maybe my breakup with Bradley fucked with my stomach." The truth: Blake Burns tasted delicious, and Bradley was the last person on my mind while my boss fucked my brains out.

"That's too bad. You missed Mel Weiner's show.

He topped last year's performance. This year he got drunk and humped the dessert table."

"Sorry I missed that." *Thank God, I did.*

"How did you get home? Chaz and I looked all over for you."

"Lip Service." Lip Service was a relatively new alternate cab service that was becoming all the rage because it was reasonable and trustworthy—even more so than popular Uber. The fleet consisted of black Nissan Cubes that bore huge red felt Mick Jagger-like lips on the front fender. All the drivers were carefully screened. By opening an account with your credit card, you could readily book a car online.

Libby folded her newspaper and placed it down on the counter. "Are you excited about going home tomorrow and seeing your parents?"

"Yes." *More than you know.*

She chugged her coffee. "I'm going to miss you."

"I'm going to miss you too.

Poor Libby was staying in town. She'd planned to travel east to see her boyfriend Everett, but at last minute, he'd been invited by one of his Oxford professors to give a lecture. I seriously didn't know how the two of them maintained their long distance relationship. But somehow it worked. Instead of getting laid, she was going to spend Christmas with her brother Chaz and a bunch of his gay friends. At least it would be fun. Tomorrow before I left, we would exchange our

Christmas presents.

Rising, my bestie put her mug into the dishwasher and then grabbed her large canvas tote bag. "Maybe I'll see you later at the office. I have to head in early. I volunteered to help with the Department Christmas breakfast. While my boss distributes bonuses to everyone, I'm handing out gifts."

Office gifts. Suddenly, I remembered I had one for Blake. Yesterday, I looked forward to giving him the little snow globe. Today, I dreaded it.

The mood in the office was upbeat and festive. Exchanges of "Merry Christmas" and "Happy Holidays" were met everywhere. Although some looked a little shitfaced from last night's party, most of my co-workers wore big smiles on their faces. The office was going to be closed for a week. Except for those with technical jobs who would be well compensated for overtime, everyone had a paid week of vacation.

I headed straight to my office and locked my door. If Blake wanted to see me, he was going to have to knock.

To my relief, he left me alone. I busied myself with a few things I wanted to wrap up before I took off. I spent a little time on the PowerPoint that I was presenting to Gloria's Secret in January and sent

"Season Greetings" e-cards to the authors I was hoping to work with in the coming year. I also watered the cactus plant that Blake had given me. I'd grown very attached to it and named it Lucky. Sitting on my credenza where it bathed in sunlight, it gave my still sterile office some life. And it brought back fond memories I wished now I could erase.

I tried hard not to think about Blake and our encounter last night. The relentless throbbing between my legs made it impossible. My eyes darted back and forth between my computer screen and the close-by snow globe. In addition to wrapping it, I'd put it into a cute little holiday gift bag with "Ho Ho Ho!" printed on it. At some point, I was going to have to give it to him.

And then my phone rang. My heart jumped. I picked it up on the first ring.

"Jennifer."

That sultry voice. It was him. Blake. My heartbeat sped up.

"I'd like you to come to my office before you leave for the day."

"I'll come now."

Come now? The double entendre sent a flurry of tingles to my core. *Get a grip, Jennifer. Stop it with all this sexual innuendo stuff. Get him out of your mind.*

"Good." He hung up the phone.

With trembling fingers, I collected his gift—better to give it to him now than having to make another trip to his office. With the bag in one hand, I smoothed my hair with the other before heading to his office. My heart was racing and so was my mind. What was I going to say to him?

That was the best sex I ever had in my life?

Thank you for the mind-blowing orgasms?

Was it as good for you as it was for me?

Shit. Shit. Shit. I had no idea. My heart was beating like a hummingbird's wings, and my stomach bubbled with nerves.

He was sitting at his desk when I traipsed into his open-door office, gazing at his computer screen. At the sound of my footsteps, he looked up at me.

"Jennifer."

"Yes?" My voice was meek.

"Have a seat."

He gestured to one of the armchairs facing his desk. He was acting like nothing had transpired between us last night. While this should have had a calming effect on me, it didn't. Angst filled my lungs like air in a balloon. And tingles pricked my body like needles. While it was "casual Friday" and I was dressed in jeans, he was impeccably dressed in one of his elegant dark suits. His smoldering blue eyes connected with mine, and he quirked one of his sexy crooked smiles. I couldn't control my reaction to him. I became acutely aware of the throbbing between my legs as my already rapid heartbeat accelerated. *Stop it, Jen. He's your boss.*

A player. It was futile. He was just too, too beautiful.

Anxiously without smiling back, I ambled toward the chair. I stumbled but luckily caught my balance before I tumbled. I silently said a Hail Mary, thankful that I didn't embarrass myself. It wasn't easy being Calamity Jen.

I lowered myself to the seat cushion as he reached for an envelope on his desk. "This is your Christmas bonus, Jennifer."

Shocked, thinking I'd not be eligible for one given that I'd worked for SIN-TV for less than a month, I took the envelope from him. My hand shook.

"Thank you," I stuttered.

He winked at me. Actually, it was more like a twitch, "Your performance has been outstanding."

My performance? My job performance or my performance last night? I dared not ask.

Nervously, I thanked him again. He was having an unnerving effect on me. My heart was pounding, and every nerve was cackling, especially the ones between my thighs. I crossed one leg over the other to contain the fiery sensations. The sooner I got out of here the better.

"What's that in your hand?" he asked, eyeing the little bag dangling from it.

I'd almost forgotten and stammered, "This is just a little something for you. Merry Christmas." I set the bag on his desk, and he instantly reached for it. My eyes stayed locked on his fingers as he took the little box out of the bag and unwrapped it. Those beautiful deft fingers that had been all over my body. Groping. Squeezing. Circling. Caressing.

That dazzling dimpled smile curled on his lips at the sight of the snow globe. He held it in his hand and admired it. The gold ball glistened.

"Thank you. I collect these." He held his eyes fierce on mine, burning a hole right through them. My raging hormones mixed with my nerves. I wanted to jump out of my skin.

I uncrossed my legs. "Well, I should be going. I've got a few last minute things to wrap up before I take off."

"Are you doing anything special over the holidays, Ms. McCoy?" His seductive tone made it sound as if he was about to proposition me.

"I'm going home to Boise to see my parents."

He nodded with approval. "Good. Sometimes getting away puts things in perspective. Makes you see things more clearly."

What was he implying? He was insinuating something in his tone.

"What about you?"

"I'm going skiing in Sun Valley. It's not too far from Boise."

I gulped. He was practically going to be in my backyard.

"Would you like to come up for a day and ski?"

I was visibly shaking. "Mr. Burns, I don't ski, and furthermore think it would be best if we don't have any contact over the break unless it's a work-related emergency."

He pressed his lips into a thin, pensive line. "I see."

Sun Valley was a playground for the rich, the beautiful, and the famous. Without warning, the thought of him spending the twelve days of Christmas with a different blond bimbo every night invaded my brain and threw my emotions into a tailspin. My breath hitched painfully in my throat.

"Are you okay, Ms. McCoy?"

I nodded wordlessly and forced myself to stand up. My legs felt like Jell-O. It took all my effort to get past the Christmas ball-sized lump in my throat and say, "Have a nice holiday, Mr. Burns." Slipping my bonus check into a skirt pocket, I turned toward the door to his office. I should have been excited about opening the envelope, but I wasn't. Unexpected sadness filled me. An emptiness that I did not want to understand.

I hadn't taken three steps when he called out to me. "Wait, Ms. McCoy. I have something for you too." I stopped dead in my tracks and pivoted around. My eyes stayed fixed on him as he lowered his head under his desk. Every muscle in my body clenched. Was he zipping down his fly? Was I about to see his colossal cock and fuck him over his desk? *Oh yes!*

Instead—and admittedly to my disappointment—he pulled out a box from under his desk. It was enormous and extravagantly wrapped with metallic green paper and an extravagant red bow.

"Come here," he said, placing it flat on his desk. I slowly made my way back to him, feeling mortified that I'd gotten him something so small and fantasized something so big in a different way.

"I don't think I should accept a gift from you," I protested meekly.

"Just open it," he ordered.

With jittery fingers, I carefully undid the exquisite wrapping. "Did you wrap this yourself?" I asked fumbling for conversation.

He rolled his eyes at me. "Are you kidding? I can't even cut a straight line. I had it professionally wrapped."

I twitched a nervous little smile as I tore off the paper. "Well, it's beautiful."

"Not as beautiful as you."

My heart skipped a beat. It was best not to respond to him.

Whatever was inside the box was rather heavy; I couldn't begin to manage what it could be. Finally unwrapping it, I lifted off the lid and peeled away a thick layer of emerald green tissue paper. My mouth fell open and my heart leapt into my throat. A loud gasp escaped.

Oh my God. I couldn't believe my eyes. It was the painting I'd admired so much at Jaime Zander's art gallery gala. His late father's erotic painting that had reduced me to tears. *The Kiss.*

"I can't take this from you," I stammered.

He smiled. "It's not returnable. Final Sale."

"Please—"

"No, I want you to have it. You need a piece of artwork to liven up that office of yours."

I stared in awe at the breathtaking abstract portrait of the artist in a passionate embrace with his wife—his muse and lover. Tears welled up in my eyes again. I brushed them away before they fell onto the canvas.

Blake's eyes met mine. I flushed with emotion. "Why are you crying, Jennifer? You should be happy. It's Christmas."

"I'm just overwhelmed," I sniffed. To say I was overwhelmed was an understatement. The memory of *his* kiss assaulted every one of my senses. Ate away at my heart. Consumed every fiber of my being. The tears kept falling.

"This is the most amazing gift I've ever gotten."

"Then enjoy it." He handed me a hankie and I dabbed my eyes with it.

"Thank you," I whispered, resisting the burning urge to throw my arms around his neck and hug him. How I longed to feel the warmth and hardness of his beautiful body. Have his delicious mouth on mine. Feel his hot cock against my belly. He nodded as if reading my mind. A long moment of silence transpired between us. The air was thick with tension and electricity.

"I'm sorry I didn't get you something bigger." My small trembling voice broke the awkward silence.

He smiled at me wistfully. "Your present is perfect. I love it." He picked up the snow globe and shook it. My eyes blinked back tears as I watched the delicate glittery flakes dance around the glimmering gold ball. A painful longing tugged at my heart.

"Then I should be going." I gathered up the box. "Enjoy your holiday, Mr. Burns."

He shot me a sexy little wink.

"You too, tiger."

With a heavy heart, I slumped out his office, not looking back or knowing what lay ahead of me.

End of THAT MAN 2

THAT MAN Trilogy

THAT MAN 3, the steamy and suspenseful conclusion to the THAT MAN trilogy, is available now.

If you enjoyed *THAT MAN 2*, I hope you will leave a short review. Reviews help others discover my books and mean so much to me.

Please join my mailing list to be notified of new releases and sales:

http://eepurl.com/N3AXb

NOTE FROM THE AUTHOR AND ACKNOWLEDGMENTS

Dearest Reader~

I actually attended the Naughty Mafia book signing event in Las Vegas, Summer 2013—the inspiration for my Vegas scenes in *That Man 2*. While I wasn't signing, it was an eye-opening experience for me to see the feverish passion attendees had for their favorite books and authors. I hope, in the near future, I will be at one of these events with a bunch of signed paperbacks. I can't wait to meet you!

I salute the world or indie erotic romance writers and wish I could turn all of their books into TV series (and maybe I will!). There are so many I've read and adored, and even more, I wish I had the time to read. And I salute all of you who support us.

Before closing, I want to thank my Beta Readers: Adriane Leigh, Cindy Meyer, Jen Oreto, Karen Lawson, and Sunshine Girl, Tracy Hogue Embert Graves. Their input was invaluable.

Thank you again for reading *THAT MAN 2*. Hope you will enjoy the conclusion to Blake and Jennifer's story.

MWAH! ~ Nelle

ABOUT THE AUTHOR

Nelle L'Amour is a *New York Times* and *USA Today* bestselling author who lives in Los Angeles with her Prince Charming-ish husband, twin teenage princesses, and a bevy of royal pain-in-the-butt pets. A former executive in the entertainment and toy industries with a prestigious Humanitus Award to her credit, she gave up playing with Barbies a long time ago but still enjoys playing with toys with her husband. While she writes in her PJs, she loves to get dressed up and pretend she's Hollywood royalty.

Nelle loves to hear from her readers.

Sign up for her newsletter: http://eepurl.com/N3AXb

Email her at: nellelamour@gmail.com

Like her on Facebook: facebook.com/NelleLamourAuthor

And connect to her on Twitter: twitter.com/nellelamour

6838438R00110

Printed in Germany
by Amazon Distribution
GmbH, Leipzig